T+SF
2.80

The Door Into Summer

Robert A. Heinlein

The Door Into Summer

Robert A. Heinlein

Doubleday & Company, Inc., Garden City, New York

All of the characters in this book are fictitious,
and any resemblance to actual persons,
living or dead, is purely coincidental.

For
A.P. and Phyllis,
Mick and Annette,
Aelurophiles All.

The Door Into Summer

I

One winter shortly before the Six Weeks War my tomcat, Petronius the Arbiter, and I lived in an old farmhouse in Connecticut. I doubt if it is there any longer, as it was near the edge of the blast area of the Manhattan near-miss, and those old frame buildings burn like tissue paper. Even if it is still standing it would not be a desirable rental because of the fall-out, but we liked it then, Pete and I. The lack of plumbing made the rent low and what had been the dining room had a good north light for my drafting board.

The drawback was that the place had eleven doors to the outside.

Twelve, if you counted Pete's door. I always tried to arrange a door of his own for Pete—in this case a board fitted into a window in an unused bedroom and in which I had cut a cat strainer just wide enough for Pete's whiskers. I have spent too much of my life opening doors for cats—I once calculated that, since the dawn of civilization, nine hundred and seventy-eight man-centuries have been used up that way. I could show you figures.

Pete usually used his own door except when he could bully me into opening a people door for him, which he preferred. But he *would not* use his door when there was snow on the ground.

While still a kitten, all fluff and buzzes, Pete had worked out a simple philosophy. I was in charge of quarters, rations, and weather; he was in charge of everything else. But he held me especially responsible for weather. Connecticut winters are good only for Christmas cards; regularly that winter Pete would check his own door, refuse to go out it because of that unpleasant white stuff beyond it (he was no fool), then badger me to open a people door.

He had a fixed conviction that at least one of them must lead into summer weather. Each time this meant that I had to go around with him to each of eleven doors, hold it open while he satisfied himself that it was winter out that way, too, then go on to the next door, while his criticisms of my mismanagement grew more bitter with each disappointment.

Then he would stay indoors until hydraulic pressure utterly forced him outside. When he returned the ice in his pads would sound like little clogs on the wooden floor and he would glare at me and refuse to purr until he had chewed it all out . . . whereupon he would forgive me until the next time.

But he never gave up his search for the Door into Summer.

On 3 December, 1970, I was looking for it too.

My quest was about as hopeless as Pete's had been in a Connecticut January. What little snow there was in southern California was kept on mountains for skiers, not in downtown Los Angeles—the stuff probably couldn't have pushed through the smog anyway. But the winter weather was in my heart.

I was not in bad health (aside from a cumulative hangover), I was still on the right side of thirty by a few days, and I was far from being broke. No police were looking for me, nor any husbands, nor any process servers; there was nothing wrong that a slight case of amnesia would not have cured. But there was winter in my heart and I was looking for the door to summer.

If I sound like a man with an acute case of self-pity, you are correct. There must have been well over two billion people on this planet in worse shape than I was. Nevertheless, I was looking for the Door into Summer.

Most of the ones I had checked lately had been swinging doors, like the pair in front of me then—the SANS SOUCI Bar Grill, the sign said. I went in, picked a booth halfway back, placed the overnight bag I was carrying carefully on the seat, slid in by it, and waited for the waiter.

The overnight bag said, "Waarrrh?"

I said, "Take it easy, Pete."

"Naaow!"

"Nonsense, you just went. Pipe down, the waiter is coming."

Pete shut up. I looked up as the waiter leaned over the table, and said to him, "A double shot of your bar Scotch, a glass of plain water, and a split of ginger ale."

The waiter looked upset. "Ginger ale, sir? With Scotch?"

"Do you have it or don't you?"

"Why, yes, of course. But——"

"Then fetch it. I'm not going to drink it; I just want to sneer at it. And bring a saucer too."

"As you say, sir." He polished the table top. "How about a small steak, sir? Or the scallops are very good today."

"Look, mate, I'll tip you for the scallops if you'll promise not to serve them. All I need is what I ordered . . . and don't forget the saucer."

He shut up and went away. I told Pete again to take it easy, the Marines had landed. The waiter returned, his pride appeased by carrying the split of ginger ale on the saucer. I had him open it while I mixed the Scotch with the water. "Would you like another glass for the ginger ale, sir?"

"I'm a real buckaroo; I drink it out of the bottle."

He shut up and let me pay him and tip him, not forgetting a tip for the scallops. When he had gone I poured ginger ale into the saucer and tapped on the top of the overnight bag. "Soup's on, Pete."

It was unzipped; I never zipped it with him inside. He spread it with his paws, poked his head out, looked around quickly, then levitated his forequarters and placed his front feet on the edge of the table. I raised my glass and we looked at each other. "Here's to the female race, Pete—find 'em and forget 'em!"

He nodded; it matched his own philosophy perfectly. He bent his head daintily and started lapping up ginger ale. "If you can, that is," I added, and took a deep swig. Pete did not answer. Forgetting a female was no effort to him; he was the natural-born bachelor type.

Facing me through the window of the bar was a sign that kept changing. First it would read: WORK WHILE YOU SLEEP. Then it would say: AND DREAM YOUR TROUBLES AWAY. Then it would flash in letters twice as big:

MUTUAL ASSURANCE COMPANY

I read all three several times without thinking about them. I knew as much and as little about suspended animation as everybody else did. I had read a popular article or so when it was first announced and two or three times a week I'd get an insurance-company ad about it in the morning mail; I usually chucked them without looking at them since they didn't seem to apply to me any more than lipstick ads did.

In the first place, until shortly before then, I could not have paid for cold sleep; it's expensive. In the second place, why should a man who was enjoying his work, was making money, expected to make more, was in love and about to be married, commit semi-suicide?

If a man had an incurable disease and expected to die anyhow but thought the doctors a generation later might be able to cure him—and he could afford to pay for suspended animation while medical science caught up with what was wrong with him—then cold sleep was a logical bet. Or if his ambition was to make a trip to Mars and he thought that clipping one generation out of his personal movie film would enable him to buy a ticket, I supposed that was logical too—there had been a news story about a café-society couple who got married and went right straight from city hall to the sleep sanctuary of Western World Insurance Company with an announcement that they had left instructions not to be called until they could spend their honeymoon on an interplanetary liner . . . although I had suspected that it was a publicity gag rigged by the insurance company and that they had ducked out the back door under assumed names. Spending your wedding night cold as a frozen mackerel does not have the ring of truth in it.

And there was the usual straightforward financial appeal, the one the insurance companies bore down on: "Work while you sleep." Just hold still and let whatever you have saved grow into a fortune. If you are fifty-five and your retirement fund pays you two hundred a month, why not sleep away the years, wake up still fifty-five, and have it pay you a thousand a month? To say nothing of waking up in a bright new world which would probably promise you a much longer and healthier old age in which to enjoy the thousand a month? That one they really went to town on, each company proving with incontrovertible figures that its selection of stocks for its trust fund made more money faster than any of the others. "Work while you sleep!"

It had never appealed to me. I wasn't fifty-five, I didn't want to retire, and I hadn't seen anything wrong with 1970.

Until recently, that is to say. Now I was retired whether I liked it or not (I didn't); instead of being on my honeymoon I was sitting in a second-rate bar drinking Scotch purely for anesthesia; instead of a wife I had one much-scarred tomcat with a neurotic taste for ginger ale; and as for liking right now, I would have swapped it for a case of gin and then busted every bottle.

But I wasn't broke.

I reached into my coat and took out an envelope, opened it. It had two items in it. One was a certified check for more money than I had ever had before at one time; the other was a stock certificate in Hired Girl, Inc. They were both getting a little mussed; I had been carrying them ever since they were handed to me.

Why not?

Why not duck out and sleep my troubles away? Pleasanter than joining the Foreign Legion, less messy than suicide, and it would divorce me completely from the events and the people who had made my life go sour. So why not?

I wasn't terribly interested in the chance to get rich. Oh, I had read H. G. Wells's *The Sleeper Awakes,* not only when the insurance companies started giving away free copies, but before that, when it was just another classic novel; I knew what compound interest and stock appreciation could do. But I was not sure that I had enough money both to buy the Long Sleep and to set up a trust large enough to be worth while. The other argument appealed to me more: go beddy-bye and wake up in a different world. Maybe a lot better world, the way the insurance companies would have you believe . . . or maybe worse. But certainly different.

I could make sure of one important difference: I could doze

long enough to be certain that it was a world without Belle Darkin—or Miles Gentry, either, but Belle especially. If Belle was dead and buried I could forget her, forget what she had done to me, cancel her out . . . instead of gnawing my heart with the knowledge that she was only a few miles away.

Let's see, how long would that have to be? Belle was twenty-three—or claimed to be (I recalled that once she had seemed to let slip that she remembered Roosevelt as President). Well, in her twenties anyhow. If I slept seventy years, she'd be an obituary. Make it seventy-five and be safe.

Then I remembered the strides they were making in geriatrics; they were talking about a hundred and twenty years as an attainable "normal" life span. Maybe I would have to sleep a hundred years. I wasn't certain that any insurance company offered that much.

Then I had a gently fiendish idea, inspired by the warm glow of Scotch. It wasn't necessary to sleep until Belle was dead; it was enough, more than enough, and just the fitting revenge on a female to be *young* when she was *old*. Just enough younger to rub her nose in it—say about thirty years.

I felt a paw, gentle as a snowflake, on my arm. "Mooorrre!" announced Pete.

"Greedy gut," I told him, and poured him another saucer of ginger ale. He thanked me with a polite wait, then started lapping it.

But he had interrupted my pleasantly nasty chain of thought. What the devil could I do about Pete?

You can't give away a cat the way you can a dog; they won't stand for it. Sometimes they go with the house, but not in Pete's case; to him I had been the one stable thing in a changing world ever since he was taken from his mother nine years earlier . . . I had even managed to keep him near me in the Army and that takes real wangling.

He was in good health and likely to stay that way even though he was held together with scar tissue. If he could just correct a tendency to lead with his right he would be winning battles and siring kittens for another five years at least.

I could pay to have him kept in a kennel until he died (unthinkable!) or I could have him chloroformed (equally unthink-

14

able)—or I could abandon him. That is what it boils down to with a cat: you either carry out the Chinese obligation you have assumed—or you abandon the poor thing, let it go wild, destroy its faith in the eternal rightness.

The way Belle had destroyed mine.

So, Danny Boy, you might as well forget it. Your own life may have gone as sour as dill pickles; that did not excuse you in the slightest from your obligation to carry out your contract to this super-spoiled cat.

Just as I reached that philosophical truth Pete sneezed; the bubbles had gone up his nose. *"Gesundheit,"* I answered, "and quit trying to drink it so fast."

Pete ignored me. His table manners averaged better than mine and he knew it. Our waiter had been hanging around the cash register, talking with the cashier. It was the after-lunch slump and the only other customers were at the bar. The waiter looked up when I said *"Gesundheit,"* and spoke to the cashier. They both looked our way, then the cashier lifted the flap gate in the bar and headed toward us.

I said quietly, "MPs, Pete."

He glanced around and ducked down into the bag; I pushed the top together. The cashier came over and leaned on my table, giving the seats on both sides of the booth a quick double-O. "Sorry, friend," he said flatly, "but you'll have to get that cat out of here."

"What cat?"

"The one you were feeding out of that saucer."

"I don't see any cat."

This time he bent down and looked under the table. "You've got him in that bag," he accused.

"Bag? Cat?" I said wonderingly. "My friend, I think you've come down with an acute figure of speech."

"Huh? Don't give me any fancy language. You've got a cat in that bag. Open it up."

"Do you have a search warrant?"

"What? Don't be silly."

"You're the one talking silly, demanding to see the inside of my bag without a search warrant. Fourth Amendment—and the war has been over for years. Now that we've settled that, please tell my waiter to make it the same all around—or fetch it yourself."

He looked pained. "Brother, this isn't anything personal, but I've got a license to consider. 'No dogs, no cats'—it says so right up there on the wall. We aim to run a sanitary establishment."

"Then your aim is poor." I picked up my glass. "See the lipstick marks? You ought to be checking your dishwasher, not searching your customers."

"I don't see no lipstick."

"I wiped most of it off. But let's take it down to the Board of Health and get the bacteria count checked."

He sighed. "You got a badge?"

"No."

"Then we're even. I don't search your bag and you don't take me down to the Board of Health. Now if you want another drink, step up to the bar and have it . . . on the house. But not here." He turned and headed up front.

I shrugged. "We were just leaving anyhow."

As I started to pass the cashier's desk on my way out he looked up. "No hard feelings?"

"Nope. But I was planning to bring my horse in here for a drink later. Now I won't."

"Suit yourself. The ordinance doesn't say a word about horses. But just one more thing—does that cat really drink ginger ale?"

"Fourth Amendment, remember?"

"I don't want to see the animal; I just want to know."

"Well," I admitted, "he prefers it with a dash of bitters, but he'll drink it straight if he has to."

"It'll ruin his kidneys. Look here a moment, friend."

"At what?"

"Lean back so that your head is close to where mine is. Now look up at the ceiling over each booth . . . the mirrors up in the decorations. I *knew* there was a cat there—because I saw it."

I leaned back and looked. The ceiling of the joint had a lot of junky decoration, including many mirrors; I saw now that a number of them, camouflaged by the design, were so angled as to permit the cashier to use them as periscopes without leaving his station. "We need that," he said apologetically. "You'd be shocked at what goes on in those booths . . . if we didn't keep an eye on 'em. It's a sad world."

"Amen, brother." I went on out.

Once outside, I opened the bag and carried it by one handle; Pete stuck his head out. "You heard what the man said, Pete. 'It's a sad world.' Worse than sad when two friends can't have a quiet drink together without being spied on. That settles it."

"Now?" asked Pete.

"If you say so. If we're going to do it, there's no point in stalling."

"Now!" Pete answered emphatically.

"Unanimous. It's right across the street."

The receptionist at the Mutual Assurance Company was a fine example of the beauty of functional design. In spite of being streamlined for about Mach Four, she displayed frontal-mounted radar housings and everything else needed for her basic mission. I reminded myself that she would be Whistler's Mother by the time I was out and told her that I wanted to see a salesman.

"Please be seated. I will see if one of our client executives is free." Before I could sit down she added, "Our Mr. Powell will see you. This way, please."

Our Mr. Powell occupied an office which made me think that Mutual did pretty well for itself. He shook hands moistly, sat me down, offered me a cigarette, and attempted to take my bag. I hung onto it. "Now, sir, how can we serve you?"

"I want the Long Sleep."

His eyebrows went up and his manner became more respectful. No doubt Mutual would write you a camera floater for seven bucks, but the Long Sleep let them get their patty-paws on *all* of a client's assets. "A very wise decision," he said reverently. "I wish I were free to take it myself. But . . . family responsibilities, you know." He reached out and picked up a form. "Sleep clients are usually in a hurry. Let me save you time and bother by filling this out for you . . . and we'll arrange for your physical examination at once."

"Just a moment."

"Eh?"

"One question. Are you set up to arrange cold sleep for a cat?"

He looked surprised, then pained. "You're jesting."

I opened the top of the bag; Pete stuck his head out. "Meet my side-kick. Just answer the question, please. If the answer is 'no,' I want to sashay up to Central Valley Liability. Their offices are in this same building, aren't they?"

This time he looked horrified. "Mister—— Uh, I didn't get your name?"

"Dan Davis."

"Mr. Davis, once a man enters our door he is under the benevolent protection of Mutual Assurance. I *couldn't* let you go to Central Valley."

"How do you plan to stop me? Judo?"

"Please!" He glanced around and looked upset. "Our company is an ethical company."

"Meaning that Central Valley is not?"

"I didn't say that; you did. Mr. Davis, don't let me sway you——"

"You won't."

"—but get sample contracts from each company. Get a lawyer, better yet, get a licensed semanticist. Find out what we offer—and actually deliver—and compare it with what Central Valley claims to offer." He glanced around again and leaned toward me. "I shouldn't say this—and I do hope you won't quote me—but they don't even use the standard actuarial tables."

"Maybe they give the customer a break instead."

"What? My dear Mr. Davis, we distribute every accrued benefit. Our charter requires it . . . while Central Valley is a stock company."

"Maybe I should buy some of their—— Look, Mr. Powell, we're wasting time. Will Mutual accept my pal here? Or not? If not, I've been here too long already."

"You mean you want to pay to have that creature preserved alive in hypothermia?"

"I mean I want both of us to take the Long Sleep. And don't call him 'that creature'; his name is Petronius."

"Sorry. I'll rephrase my question. You are prepared to pay two custodial fees to have both of you, you and, uh, Petronius committed to our sanctuary?"

"Yes. But not two standard fees. Something extra, of course, but you can stuff us both in the same coffin; you can't honestly charge as much for Pete as you charge for a man."

"This is most unusual."

"Of course it is. But we'll dicker over the price later . . . or I'll dicker with Central Valley. Right now I want to find out if you can do it."

18

"Uh . . ." He drummed on his desk top. "Just a moment." He picked up his phone and said, "Opal, get me Dr. Berquist." I didn't hear the rest of the conversation, for he switched on the privacy guard. But after a while he put down the instrument and smiled as if a rich uncle had died. "Good news, sir! I had overlooked momentarily the fact that the first successful experiments were made on cats. The techniques and critical factors for cats are fully established. In fact there is a cat at the Naval Research Laboratory in Annapolis which is and has been for more than twenty years alive in hypothermia."

"I thought NRL was wiped out when they got Washington?"

"Just the surface buildings, sir, not the deep vaults. Which is a tribute to the perfection of the technique; the animal was unattended save by automatic machinery for more than two years . . . yet it still lives, unchanged, unaged. As you will live, sir, for whatever period you elect to entrust yourself to Mutual."

I thought he was going to cross himself. "Okay, okay, now let's get on with the dicker."

There were four factors involved: first, how to pay for our care while we were hibernating; second, how long I wanted us to sleep; third, how I wanted my money invested while I was in the freezer; and last, what happened if I conked out and never woke up.

I finally settled on the year 2000, a nice round number and only thirty years away. I was afraid that if I made it any longer I would be completely out of touch. The changes in the last thirty years (my own lifetime) had been enough to bug a man's eyes out—two big wars and a dozen little ones, the downfall of communism, the Great Panic, the artificial satellites, the change to atomic power—why, when I was a kid they didn't even have multimorphs.

I might find 2000 A.D. pretty confusing. But if I didn't jump that far Belle would not have time to work up a fancy set of wrinkles.

When it came to how to invest my dough I did not consider government bonds and other conservative investments; our fiscal system has inflation built into it. I decided to hang onto my Hired Girl stock and put the cash into other common stocks, with a special eye to some trends I thought would grow. Automation was bound to get bigger. I picked a San Francisco fertilizer firm too; it had been experimenting with yeasts and edible algae—there were more people every year and steak wasn't going to get any cheaper. The balance of the money I told him to put into the company's managed trust fund.

But the real choice lay in what to do if I died in hibernation. The company claimed that the odds were better than seven out of ten that I would live through thirty years of cold sleep . . . and the company would take either end of the bet. The odds weren't reciprocal and I didn't expect them to be; in any honest gambling there is a breakage to the house. Only crooked gamblers claim to give the sucker the best of it, and insurance is legalized gambling. The oldest and most reputable insurance firm in the world, Lloyd's of London, makes no bones about it—Lloyd's associates will take either end of any bet. But don't expect better-than-track odds; somebody has to pay for Our Mr. Powell's tailor-made suits.

I chose to have every cent go to the company trust fund in case I died . . . which made Mr. Powell want to kiss me and made me wonder just how optimistic those seven-out-of-ten odds were. But I stuck with it because it made me an heir (if I lived) of everyone else with the same option (if they died), Russian roulette with the survivors picking up the chips . . . and with the company, as usual, raking in the house percentage.

I picked every alternative for the highest possible return and no hedging if I guessed wrong; Mr. Powell loved me, the way a croupier loves a sucker who keeps playing the zero. By the time we had settled my estate he was anxious to be reasonable about Pete; we settled for 15 per cent of the human fee to pay for Pete's hibernation and drew up a separate contract for him.

There remained consent of court and the physical examination. The physical I didn't worry about; I had a hunch that, once I elected to have the company bet that I would die, they would accept me even in the last stages of the Black Death. But I thought that getting a judge to okay it might be lengthy. It had to be done, because a client in cold sleep was legally in chancery, alive but helpless.

I needn't have worried. Our Mr. Powell had quadruplicate originals made of nineteen different papers. I signed till I got finger cramps, and a messenger rushed away with them while I went to my physical examination; I never even saw the judge.

The physical was the usual tiresome routine except for one thing. Toward the end the examining physician looked me sternly in the eye and said, "Son, how long have you been on this binge?"

"Binge?"

"Binge."

"What makes you think that, Doctor? I'm as sober as you are. 'Peter Piper picked a peck of pickled——'"

"Knock it off and answer me."

"Mmm . . . I'd say about two weeks. A little over."

"Compulsive drinker? How many times have you pulled this stunt in the past?"

"Well, as a matter of fact, I haven't. You see——" I started to tell him what Belle and Miles had done to me, why I felt the way I did.

He shoved a palm at me. "Please. I've got troubles of my own and I'm not a psychiatrist. Really, all I'm interested in is finding out whether or not your heart will stand up under the ordeal of putting you down to four degrees centigrade. Which it will. And I ordinarily don't care why anyone is nutty enough to crawl into a hole and pull it in after him; I just figure it is one less damn fool underfoot. But some residual tinge of professional conscience prevents me from letting any man, no matter how sorry a specimen, climb into one of those coffins while his brain is sodden with alcohol. Turn around."

"Huh?"

"Turn around; I'm going to inject you in your left buttock." I did and he did. While I was rubbing it he went on, "Now drink this. In about twenty minutes you will be more sober than you've been in a month. Then, if you have any sense—which I doubt—you can review your position and decide whether to run away from your troubles . . . or stand up to them like a man."

I drank it.

"That's all; you can get dressed. I'm signing your papers, but I'm warning you that I can veto it right up to the last minute. No more alcohol for you at all, a light supper and no breakfast. Be here at noon tomorrow for final check."

He turned away and didn't even say good-by. I dressed and

went out of there, sore as a boil. Powell had all my papers ready. When I picked them up he said, "You can leave them here if you wish and pick them up at noon tomorrow . . . the set that goes in the vault with you, that is."

"What happens to the others?"

"We keep one set ourselves, then after you are committed we file one set with the court and one in the Carlsbad Archives. Uh, did the doctor caution you about diet?"

"He certainly did." I glanced at the papers to cover my annoyance.

Powell reached for them. "I'll keep them safe overnight."

I pulled them back. "I can keep them safe. I might want to change some of these stock selections."

"Uh, it's rather late for that, my dear Mr. Davis."

"Don't rush me. If I do make any changes I'll come in early." I opened the overnight bag and stuck the papers down in a side flap beside Pete. I had kept valuable papers there before; while it might not be as safe as the public archives in the Carlsbad Caverns, they were safer than you might think. A sneak thief had tried to take something out of that flap on another occasion; he must still have the scars of Pete's teeth and claws.

II

My car was parked under Pershing Square where I had left it earlier in the day. I dropped money into the parking attendant, set the bug on arterial-west, got Pete out and put him on the seat, and relaxed.

Or tried to relax. Los Angeles traffic was too fast and too slashingly murderous for me to be really happy under automatic control; I wanted to redesign their whole installation—it was not a really modern "fail safe." By the time we were west of Western Avenue and could go back on manual control I was edgy and wanted a drink. "There's an oasis, Pete."

"Blurrrt?"

"Right ahead."

But while I was looking for a place to park—Los Angeles was safe from invasion; the invaders wouldn't find a place to park—I recalled the doctor's order not to touch alcohol.

So I told him emphatically what he could do with his orders.

Then I wondered if he could tell, almost a day later, whether or not I had taken a drink. I seemed to recall some technical article, but it had not been in my line and I had just skimmed it.

Damnation, he was quite capable of refusing to let me cold-sleep. I'd better play it cagey and lay off the stuff.

"Now?" inquired Pete.

"Later. We're going to find a drive-in instead." I suddenly realized that I didn't really want a drink; I wanted food and a night's sleep. Doc was correct; I was more sober and felt better than I had in weeks. Mabye that shot in the fanny had been nothing but B_1; if so, it was jet-propelled. So we found a drive-in restaurant. I ordered chicken in the rough for me and a half pound of hamburger and some milk for Pete and took him out for a short walk while it was coming. Pete and I ate in drive-ins a lot because I didn't have to sneak him in and out.

A half hour later I let the car drift back out of the busy circle, stopped it, lit a cigarette, scratched Pete under the chin, and thought.

Dan, my boy, the doc was right; you've been trying to dive down the neck of a bottle. That's okay for your pointy head but it's too narrow for your shoulders. Now you're cold sober, you've got your belly crammed with food and it's resting comfortably for the first time in days. You feel better.

What else? Was the doc right about the rest of it? Are you a spoiled infant? Do you lack the guts to stand up to a setback? Why are you taking this step? Is it the spirit of adventure? Or are you simply hiding from yourself, like a Section Eight trying to crawl back into his mother's womb?

But I *do* want to do it, I told myself—the year 2000. Boy!

Okay, so you want to. But do you have to run off without settling the beefs you have right here?

All right, all right!—but *how* can I settle them? I don't want Belle back, not after what she's done. And what else can I do? Sue them? Don't be silly, I've got no evidence—and anyhow, nobody ever wins a lawsuit but the lawyers.

Pete said, "Wellll? Y'know!"

I looked down at his waffle-scarred head. Pete wouldn't sue anybody; if he didn't like the cut of another cat's whiskers, he simply invited him to come out and fight like a cat. "I believe you're right, Pete. I'm going to look up Miles, tear his arm off, and beat him over the head with it until he talks. We can take the Long Sleep afterward. But we've got to know just what it was they did to us and who rigged it."

There was a phone booth back of the stand. I called Miles, found him at home, and told him to stay there; I'd be out.

24

My old man named me Daniel Boone Davis, which was his way of declaring for personal liberty and self-reliance. I was born in 1940, a year when everybody was saying that the individual was on the skids and the future belonged to mass man. Dad refused to believe it; naming me was a note of defiance. He died under brainwashing in North Korea, trying to the last to prove his thesis.

When the Six Weeks War came along I had a degree in mechanical engineering and was in the Army. I had not used my degree to try for a commission because the one thing Dad had left me was an overpowering yen to be on my own, giving no orders, taking no orders, keeping no schedules—I simply wanted to serve my hitch and get out. When the Cold War boiled over, I was a sergeant-technician at Sandia Weapons Center in New Mexico, stuffing atoms in atom bombs and planning what I would do when my time was up. The day Sandia disappeared I was down in Dallas drawing a fresh supply of *Schrecklichkeit*. The fall-out on that was toward Oklahoma City, so I lived to draw my GI benefits.

Pete lived through it for a similar reason. I had a buddy, Miles Gentry, a veteran called back to duty. He had married a widow with one daughter, but his wife had died about the time he was called back. He lived off post with a family in Albuquerque so as to have a home for his stepchild Frederica. Little Ricky (we never called her "Frederica") took care of Pete for me. Thanks to the cat-goddess Bubastis, Miles and Ricky and Pete were away on a seventy-two that awful weekend—Ricky took Pete with them because I could not take him to Dallas.

I was as surprised as anyone when it turned out we had divisions stashed away at Thule and other places that no one suspected. It had been known since the '30s that the human body could be chilled until it slowed down to almost nothing. But it had been a laboratory trick, or a last-resort therapy, until the Six Weeks War. I'll say this for military research: if money and men can do it, it gets results. Print another billion, hire another thousand scientists and engineers, then in some incredible, left-handed, inefficient fashion the answers come up. Stasis, cold sleep, hibernation, hypothermia, reduced metabolism, call it what you will—the logistics-medicine research teams had found a way to stack people like

25

cordwood and use them when needed. First you drug the subject, then hypnotize him, then cool him down and hold him precisely at four degrees centigrade; that is to say, at the maximum density of water with no ice crystals. If you need him in a hurry he can be brought up by diathermy and posthypnotic command in ten minutes (they did it in seven at Nome), but such speed tends to age the tissues and may make him a little stupid from then on. If you aren't in a hurry two hours minimum is better. The quick method is what professional soldiers call a "calculated risk."

The whole thing was a risk the enemy had not calculated, so when the war was over I was paid off instead of being liquidated or sent to a slave camp, and Miles and I went into business together about the time the insurance companies started selling cold sleep.

We went to the Mojave Desert, set up a small factory in an Air Force surplus building, and started making *Hired Girl*, my engineering and Miles's law and business experience. Yes, I invented *Hired Girl* and all her kinfolk—*Window Willie* and the rest—even though you won't find my name on them. While I was in the service I had thought hard about what one engineer can do. Go to work for Standard, or du Pont, or General Motors? Thirty years later they give you a testimonial dinner and a pension. You haven't missed any meals, you've had a lot of rides in company airplanes. But you are never your own boss. The other big market for engineers is civil service—good starting pay, good pensions, no worries, thirty days annual leave, liberal benefits. But I had just had a long government vacation and wanted to be my own boss.

What was there small enough for one engineer and not requiring six million man-hours before the first model was on the market? Bicycle-shop engineering with peanuts for capital, the way Ford and the Wright brothers had started—people said those days were gone forever; I didn't believe it.

Automation was booming—chemical-engineering plants that required only two gauge-watchers and a guard, machines that printed tickets in one city and marked the space "sold" in six other cities, steel moles that mined coal while the UMW boys sat back and watched. So while I was on Uncle Sam's payroll I soaked up all the electronics, linkages, and cybernetics that a "Q" clearance would permit.

What was the last thing to go automatic? Answer: any housewife's house. I didn't attempt to figure out a sensible scientific house; women didn't want one; they simply wanted a better-upholstered cave. But housewives were still complaining about the Servant Problem long after servants had gone the way of the mastodon. I had rarely met a housewife who did not have a touch of slaveholder in her; they seemed to think there really *ought* to be strapping peasant girls grateful for a chance to scrub floors fourteen hours a day and eat table scraps at wages a plumber's helper would scorn.

That's why we called the monster *Hired Girl*—it brought back thoughts of the semi-slave immigrant girl whom Grandma used to bully. Basically it was just a better vacuum cleaner and we planned to market it at a price competitive with ordinary suck brooms.

What *Hired Girl* would do (the first model, not the semi-intelligent robot I developed it into) was to clean floors . . . any floor, all day long and without supervision. And there never was a floor that didn't need cleaning.

It swept, or mopped, or vacuum-cleaned, or polished, consulting tapes in its idiot memory to decide which. Anything larger than a BB shot it picked up and placed in a tray on its upper surface, for someone brighter to decide whether to keep or throw away. It went quietly looking for dirt all day long, in search curves that could miss nothing, passing over clean floors in its endless search for dirty floors. It would get out of a room with people in it, like a well-trained maid, unless its mistress caught up with it and flipped a switch to tell the poor thing it was welcome. Around dinnertime it would go to its stall and soak up a quick charge—this was before we installed the everlasting power pack.

There was not too much difference between *Hired Girl*, Mark One, and a vacuum cleaner. But the difference—that it would clean without supervision—was enough; it sold.

I swiped the basic prowl pattern from the "Electric Turtles" that were written up in *Scientific American* in the late forties, lifted a memory circuit out of the brain of a guided missile (that's the nice thing about top-secret gimmicks; they don't get patented), and I took the cleaning devices and linkages out of a dozen things, including a floor polisher used in army hospitals, a soft-drink dispenser, and those "hands" they use in atomics plants to handle anything "hot." There wasn't anything really new in it; it was just the way I put it together. The "spark of genius" required by our laws lay in getting a good patent lawyer.

The real genius was in the production engineering; the whole thing could be built with standard parts ordered out of Sweet's Catalogue, with the exception of two three-dimensional cams and one printed circuit. The circuit we subcontracted; the cams I made myself in the shed we called our "factory," using war-surplus automated tools. At first Miles and I were the whole assembly line —bash to fit, file to hide, paint to cover. The pilot model cost $4317.09; the first hundred cost just over $39 each—and we passed them on to a Los Angeles discount house at $60 and they sold them for $85. We had to let them go on consignment to unload them at all, since we could not afford sales promotion, and we darn near starved before receipts started coming in. Then *Life* ran a two-page on *Hired Girl* . . . and it was a case of having enough help to assemble the monster.

Belle Darkin joined us soon after that. Miles and I had been pecking out letters on a 1908 Underwood; we hired her as a typewriter jockey and bookkeeper and rented an electric machine with executive type face and carbon ribbon and I designed a letterhead. We were ploughing it all back into the business and Pete and I were sleeping in the shop while Miles and Ricky had a nearby shack. We incorporated in self-defense. It takes three to incorporate; we gave Belle a share of stock and designated her secretary-treasurer. Miles was president and general manager; I was chief engineer and chairman of the board . . . with 51 per cent of the stock.

I want to make clear why I kept control. I wasn't a hog; I simply wanted to be my own boss. Miles worked like a trouper, I give him credit. But better than 60 per cent of the savings that got us started were mine and 100 per cent of the inventiveness and engineering were mine. Miles could not possibly have built *Hired Girl,* whereas I could have built it with any of a dozen partners, or possibly without one—although I might have flopped in trying to make money out of it; Miles was a businessman while I am not.

But I wanted to be certain that I retained control of the shop —and I granted Miles equal freedom in the business end . . . too much freedom, it turned out.

Hired Girl, Mark One, was selling like beer at a ball game and I was kept busy for a while improving it and setting up a real assembly line and putting a shop master in charge, then I happily turned to thinking up more household gadgets. Amazingly little real thought had been given to housework, even though it is at least 50 per cent of all work in the world. The women's magazines talked about "labor saving in the home" and "functional kitchens," but it was just prattle; their pretty pictures showed living-working arrangements essentially no better than those in Shakespeare's day; the horse-to-jet-plane revolution had not reached the home.

I stuck to my conviction that housewives were reactionaries. No "machines for living"—just gadgets to replace the extinct domestic servant, that is, for cleaning and cooking and baby tending.

I got to thinking about dirty windows and that ring around the bathtub that is so hard to scrub, as you have to bend double to get at it. It turned out that an electrostatic device could make dirt go *spung!* off any polished silica surface, window glass, bathtubs, toilet bowls—anything of that sort. That was *Window Willie* and it's a wonder that somebody hadn't thought of him sooner. I held him back until I had him down to a price that people could not refuse. Do you know what window washing used to cost by the hour?

I held *Willie* out of production much longer than suited Miles. He wanted to sell it as soon as it was cheap enough, but I insisted on one more thing: *Willie* had to be easy to repair. The great shortcoming of most household gadgets was that the better they were and the more they did, the more certain they were to get out of order when you needed them most—and then require an expert at five dollars an hour to make them move again. Then the same thing will happen the following week, if not to the dishwasher, then to the air conditioner . . . usually late Saturday night during a snowstorm.

I wanted my gadgets to work and keep on working and not to cause ulcers in their owners.

But gadgets do get out of order, even mine. Until that great day when all gadgets are designed with no moving parts, machinery will continue to go sour. If you stuff a house with gadgets some of them will always be out of order.

But military research does get results and the military had licked this problem years earlier. You simply can't lose a battle, lose thousands or millions of lives, maybe the war itself, just because some gadget the size of your thumb breaks down. For military purposes they used a lot of dodges—"fail safe," stand-by circuits, "tell me three times," and so forth. But one they used that made sense for household equipment was the plug-in component principle.

It is a moronically simple idea: don't repair, replace. I wanted to make every part of *Window Willie* which could go wrong a plug-in unit, then include a set of replacements with each *Willie*. Some components would be thrown away, some would be sent out for repair, but *Willie* himself would never break down longer than necessary to plug in the replacement part.

Miles and I had our first row. I said the decision as to when to go from pilot model to production was an engineering one; he claimed that it was a business decision. If I hadn't retained control *Willie* would have gone on the market just as maddeningly subject to acute appendicitis as all other sickly, half-engineered "labor-saving" gadgets.

Belle Darkin smoothed over the row. If she had turned on the pressure I might have let Miles start selling *Willie* before I thought it was ready, for I was as goofed up about Belle as is possible for a man to be.

Belle was not only a perfect secretary and office manager, she also had personal specs which would have delighted Praxiteles and a fragrance which affected me the way catnip does Pete. With top-notch office girls as scarce as they were, when one of the best turns out to be willing to work for a shoestring company at a below-standard salary, one really ought to ask "why?"—but we didn't even ask where she had worked last, so happy were we to have her dig us out of the flood of paper work that marketing *Hired Girl* had caused.

30

Later on I would have indignantly rejected any suggestion that we should have checked on Belle, for by then her bust measurement had seriously warped my judgment. She let me explain how lonely my life had been until she came along and she answered gently that she would have to know me better but that she was inclined to feel the same way.

Shortly after she smoothed out the quarrel between Miles and myself she agreed to share my fortunes. "Dan darling, you have it in you to be a great man . . . and I have hopes that I am the sort of woman who can help you."

"You certainly are!"

"Shush, darling. But I am not going to marry you right now and burden you with kids and worry you to death. I'm going to work with you and build up the business first. Then we'll get married."

I objected, but she was firm. "No, darling. We are going a long way, you and I. *Hired Girl* will be as great a name as General Electric. But when we marry I want to forget business and just devote myself to making you happy. But first I must devote myself to your welfare and your future. Trust me, dear."

So I did. She wouldn't let me buy her the expensive engagement ring I wanted to buy; instead I signed over to her some of my stock as a betrothal present. I went on voting it, of course. Thinking back, I'm not sure who thought of that present.

I worked harder than ever after that, thinking about wastebaskets that would empty themselves and a linkage to put dishes away after the dishwasher was through. Everybody was happy . . . everybody but Pete and Ricky, that is. Pete ignored Belle, as he did anything he disapproved of but could not change, but Ricky was really unhappy.

My fault. Ricky had been "my girl" since she was a six-year-old at Sandia, with hair ribbons and big solemn dark eyes. I was "going to marry her" when she grew up and we would both take care of Pete. I thought it was a game we were playing, and perhaps it was, with little Ricky serious only to the extent that it offered her eventual full custody of our cat. But how can you tell what goes on in a child's mind?

I am not sentimental about kids. Little monsters, most of them, who don't civilize until they are grown and sometimes not then.

31

But little Frederica reminded me of my own sister at that age, and besides, she liked Pete and treated him properly. I think she liked me because I never talked down (I had resented that myself as a child) and took her Brownie activities seriously. Ricky was okay; she had quiet dignity and was not a banger, not a squealer, not a lap climber. We were friends, sharing the responsibility for Pete, and, so far as I knew, her being "my girl" was just a sophisticated game we were playing.

I quit playing it after my sister and mother got it the day they bombed us. No conscious decision—I just didn't feel like joking and never went back to it. Ricky was seven then; she was ten by the time Belle joined us and possibly eleven when Belle and I became engaged. She hated Belle with an intensity that I think only I was aware of, since it was expressed only by reluctance to talk to her—Belle called it "shyness" and I think Miles thought it was too.

But I knew better and tried to talk Ricky out of it. Did you ever try to discuss with a subadolescent something the child does not want to talk about? You'll get more satisfaction shouting in Echo Canyon. I told myself it would wear off as Ricky learned how very lovable Belle was.

Pete was another matter, and if I had not been in love I would have seen it as a clear sign that Belle and I would never understand each other. Belle "liked" my cat—oh, sure, sure! She adored cats and she loved my incipient bald spot and admired my choice in restaurants and she liked everything about me.

But liking cats is hard to fake to a cat person. There are cat people and there are others, more than a majority probably, who "cannot abide a harmless, necessary cat." If they try to pretend, out of politeness or any reason, it shows, because they don't understand how to treat cats—and cat protocol is more rigid than that of diplomacy.

It is based on self-respect and mutual respect and it has the same flavor as the *dignidad de hombre* of Latin America which you may offend only at risk to your life.

Cats have no sense of humor, they have terribly inflated egos, and they are very touchy. If somebody asked me why it was worth anyone's time to cater to them I would be forced to answer that there is no logical reason. I would rather explain to someone who detests sharp cheeses why he "ought to like" Limburger. Nevertheless, I fully sympathize with the mandarin who cut off a priceless embroidered sleeve because a kitten was sleeping on it.

Belle tried to show that she "liked" Pete by treating him like a dog . . . so she got scratched. Then, being a sensible cat, he got out in a hurry and stayed out a long time—which was well, as I would have smacked him, and Pete has never been smacked, not by me. Hitting a cat is worse than useless; a cat can be disciplined only by patience, never by blows.

So I put iodine on Belle's scratches, then tried to explain what she had done wrong. "I'm sorry it happened—I'm terribly sorry! But it will happen again if you do that again."

"But I was just petting him!"

"Uh, yes . . . but you weren't cat-petting him; you were dog-petting him. You must never pat a cat, you stroke it. You must never make sudden movements in range of its claws. You must never touch it without giving it a chance to see that you are about to . . . and you must always watch to see that it likes it. If it doesn't want to be petted, it will put up with a little out of politeness—cats are very polite—but you can tell if it is merely enduring it and stop before its patience is exhausted." I hesitated. "You don't like cats, do you?"

"What? Why, how silly! Of course I like cats." But she added, "I haven't been around them much, I suppose. She's pretty touchy, isn't she?"

" 'He.' Pete is a he-male cat. No, actually he's not touchy, since he's always been well treated. But you do have to learn how to behave with cats. Uh, you must never laugh at them."

"What? Forevermore, *why?*"

"Not because they aren't funny; they're extremely comical. But they have no sense of humor and it offends them. Oh, a cat won't scratch you for laughing; he'll simply stalk off and you'll have trouble making friends with him. But it's not too important. Knowing how to pick up a cat is much more important. When Pete comes back in I'll show you how."

But Pete didn't come back in, not then, and I never showed her. Belle didn't touch him after that. She spoke to him and acted as if she liked him, but she kept her distance and he kept his. I put it out of my mind; I couldn't let so trivial a thing make me doubt the woman who was more to me than anything in life.

But the subject of Pete almost reached a crisis later. Belle and I were discussing where we were going to live. She still wouldn't set the date, but we spent a lot of time on such details. I wanted a ranchette near the plant; she favored a flat in town until we could afford a Bel-Air estate.

I said, "Darling, it's not practical; I've got to be near the plant. Besides, did you ever try to take care of a tomcat in a city apartment?"

"Oh, that! Look, darling, I'm glad you mentioned it. I've been studying up on cats, I really have. We'll have him altered. Then he'll be much gentler and perfectly happy in a flat."

I stared at her, unable to believe my ears. Make a eunuch of that old warrior? Change him into a fireside decoration? "Belle, you don't know what you're saying!"

She tut-tutted me with the old familiar "Mother knows best," giving the stock arguments of people who mistake cats for property . . . how it wouldn't hurt him, that it was really for his own good, how she knew how much I valued him and she would never think of depriving me of him, how it was really very simple and quite safe and better for everybody.

I cut in on her. "Why don't you arrange it for both of us?"

"What, dear?"

"Me, too. I'd be much more docile and I'd stay home nights and I'd never argue with you. As you pointed out, it doesn't hurt and I'd probably be a lot happier."

She turned red. "You're being preposterous."

"So are you!"

She never mentioned it again. Belle never let a difference of opinion degenerate into a row; she shut up and bided her time. But she never gave up, either. In some ways she had a lot of cat in her . . . which may have been why I couldn't resist her.

I was glad to drop the matter. I was up to here in *Flexible Frank*. *Willie* and *Hired Girl* were bound to make us lots of money, but I had a bee in my bonnet about the perfect, all-work household automaton, the general-purpose servant. All right, call it a robot, though that is a much-abused word and I had no notion of building a mechanical man.

I wanted a gadget which could do *anything* inside the home—

cleaning and cooking, of course, but also really hard jobs, like changing a baby's diaper, or replacing a typewriter ribbon. Instead of a stable of *Hired Girls* and *Window Willies* and *Nursemaid Nans* and *Houseboy Harries* and *Gardener Guses* I wanted a man and wife to be able to buy one machine for, oh, say about the price of a good automobile, which would be the equal of the Chinese servant you read about but no one in my generation had ever seen.

If I could do that it would be the Second Emancipation Proclamation, freeing women from their age-old slavery. I wanted to abolish the old saw about how "women's work is never done." Housekeeping is repetitious and unnecessary drudgery; as an engineer it offended me.

For the problem to be within the scope of one engineer, almost all of *Flexible Frank* had to be standard parts and must not involve any new principles. Basic research is no job for one man alone; this had to be development from former art or I couldn't do it.

Fortunately there was an awful lot of former art in engineering and I had not wasted my time while under a "Q" clearance. What I wanted wasn't as complicated as the things a guided missile was required to do.

Just what did I want *Flexible Frank* to do? Answer: any work a human being does around a house. He didn't have to play cards, make love, eat, or sleep, but he did have to clean up after the card game, cook, make beds, and tend babies—at least he had to keep track of a baby's breathing and call someone if it changed. I decided he did not have to answer telephone calls, as A.T.&T. was already renting a gadget for that. There was no need for him to answer the door either, as most new houses were being equipped with door answerers.

But to do the multitude of things I wanted him to do, he had to have hands, eyes, ears, and a brain . . . a good enough brain.

Hands I could order from the atomics-engineering equipment companies who supplied *Hired Girl's* hands, only this time I would want the best, with wide-range servos and with the delicate feedback required for microanalysis manipulations and for weighing radioactive isotopes. The same companies could supply eyes—only they could be simpler, since *Frank* would not have to see and manipulate from behind yards of concrete shielding the way they do in a reactor plant.

The ears I could buy from any of a dozen radio-TV houses—though I might have to do some circuit designing to have his hands controlled simultaneously by sight, sound, and touch feedback the way the human hand is controlled.

But you can do an awful lot in a small space with transistors and printed circuits.

Frank wouldn't have to use stepladders. I would make his neck stretch like an ostrich and his arms extend like lazy tongs. Should I make him able to go up and down stairs?

Well, there was a powered wheel chair that could. Maybe I should buy one and use it for the chassis, limiting the pilot model to a space no bigger than a wheel chair and no heavier than such a chair could carry—that would give me a set of parameters. I'd tie its power and steering into *Frank's* brain.

The brain was the real hitch. You can build a gadget linked like a man's skeleton or even much better. You can give it a feedback-control system good enough to drive nails, scrub floors, crack eggs—or not crack eggs. But unless it has that stuff between the ears that a man has, it is not a man, it's not even a corpse.

Fortunately I didn't need a human brain; I just wanted a docile moron, capable of largely repetitive household jobs.

Here is where the Thorsen memory tubes came in. The intercontinental missiles we had struck back with "thought" with Thorsen tubes, and traffic-control systems in places like Los Angeles used an idiot form of them. No need to go into theory of an electronic tube that even Bell Labs doesn't understand too well, the point is that you can hook a Thorsen tube into a control circuit, direct the machine through an operation by manual control, and the tube will "remember" what was done and can direct the operation *without* a human supervisor a second time, or any number of times. For an automated machine tool this is enough; for guided missiles and for *Flexible Frank* you add side circuits that give the machine "judgment." Actually it isn't judgment (in my opinion a machine can never have judgment); the side circuit is a hunting circuit, the programming of which says "look for so-and-so within such-and-such limits; when you find it, carry out your basic instruction." The basic instruction can be as complicated as you can crowd into one Thorsen memory tube—which is a *very* wide limit indeed!—and you can program so that your "judgment" circuits (moronic back-seat drivers, they are) can interrupt the basic instructions any time the cycle does not match that originally impressed into the Thorsen tube.

This meant that you need cause *Flexible Frank* to clear the table and scrape the dishes and load them into the dishwasher only once, and from then on he could cope with any dirty dishes he ever encountered. Better still, he could have an electronically duplicated Thorsen tube stuck into his head and could handle dirty dishes the first time he ever encountered them . . . and never break a dish.

Stick another "memorized" tube alongside the first one and he could change a wet baby first time, and never, never, never stick a pin in the baby.

Frank's square head could easily hold a hundred Thorsen tubes, each with an electronic "memory" of a different household task. Then throw a guard circuit around all the "judgment" circuits, a circuit which required him to hold still and squawl for help if he ran into something not covered by his instructions—that way you wouldn't use up babies or dishes.

So I did build *Frank* on the framework of a powered wheel chair. He looked like a hatrack making love to an octopus . . . but, boy, how he could polish silverware!

Miles looked over the first *Frank,* watched him mix a martini and serve it, then go around emptying and polishing ash trays (never touching ones that were clean), open a window and fasten it open, then go to my bookcase and dust and tidy the books in it. Miles took a sip of his martini and said, "Too much vermouth."

"It's the way I like them. But we can tell him to fix yours one way and mine another; he's got plenty of blank tubes in him. Flexible."

Miles took another sip. "How soon can he be engineered for production?"

"Uh, I'd like to fiddle with him for about ten years." Before he could groan I added, "But we ought to be able to put a limited model into production in five."

"Nonsense! We'll get you plenty of help and have a Model-T job ready in six months."

"The devil you will. This is my magnum opus. I'm not going to turn him loose until he is a work of art . . . about a third that size, everything plug-in replaceable but the Thorsens, and so all-out flexible that he'll not only wind the cat and wash the baby, he'll even play ping-pong if the buyer wants to pay for the extra programming." I looked at him; *Frank* was quietly dusting my desk and putting every paper back exactly where he found it. "But ping-pong with him wouldn't be much fun; he'd never miss. No, I suppose we could teach him to miss with a random-choice circuit. Mmm . . . yes, we could. We will, it would make a nice selling demonstration."

"One year, Dan, and not a day over. I'm going to hire somebody away from Loewy to help you with the styling."

I said, "Miles, when are you going to learn that I boss the engineering? Once I turn him over to you, he's yours . . . but not a split second before."

Miles answered, "It's still too much vermouth."

I piddled along with the help of the shop mechanics until I had *Frank* looking less like a three-car crash and more like something you might want to brag about to the neighbors. In the meantime I smoothed a lot of bugs out of his control system. I even taught him to stroke Pete and scratch him under his chin in such a fashion that Pete liked it—and, believe me, that takes negative feedback as exact as anything used in atomics labs. Miles didn't crowd me, although he came in from time to time and watched the progress. I did most of my work at night, coming back after dinner with Belle and taking her home. Then I would sleep most of the day, arrive late in the afternoon, sign whatever papers Belle had for me, see what the shop had done during the day, then take Belle out to dinner again. I didn't try to do much before then, because creative work makes a man stink like a goat. After a hard night in the lab shop nobody could stand me but Pete.

Just as we were finishing dinner one day Belle said to me, "Going back to the shop, dear?"

"Sure. Why not?"

"Good. Because Miles is going to meet us there."

"Huh?"

"He wants a stockholders' meeting."

"A stockholders' meeting? Why?"

"It won't take long. Actually, dear, you haven't been paying much attention to the firm's business lately. Miles wants to gather up loose ends and settle some policies."

"I've been sticking close to the engineering. What else am I supposed to do for the firm?"

"Nothing, dear. Miles says it won't take long."

"What's the trouble? Can't Jake handle the assembly line?"

"Please, dear. Miles didn't tell me why. Finish your coffee."

Miles was waiting for us at the plant and shook hands as solemnly as if we had not met in a month. I said, "Miles, what's this all about?"

He turned to Belle. "Get the agenda, will you?" This alone should have told me that Belle had been lying when she claimed that Miles had not told her what he had in mind. But I did not think of it—hell, I *trusted* Belle!—and my attention was distracted by something else, for Belle went to the safe, spun the knob, and opened it.

I said, "By the way, dear, I tried to open that last night and couldn't. Have you changed the combination?"

She was hauling papers out and did not turn. "Didn't I tell you? The patrol asked me to change it after that burglar scare last week."

"Oh. You'd better give me the new numbers or some night I'll have to phone one of you at a ghastly hour."

"Certainly." She closed the safe and put a folder on the table we used for conferences.

Miles cleared his throat and said, "Let's get started."

I answered, "Okay. Darling, if this is a formal meeting, I guess you had better make pothooks. . . . Uh, Wednesday, November eighteenth, 1970, 9:20 P.M., all stockholders present—put our names down—D. B. Davis, chairman of the board and presiding. Any old business?"

There wasn't any. "Okay, Miles, it's your show. Any new business?"

Miles cleared his throat. "I want to review the firm's policies,

39

present a program for the future, and have the board consider a financing proposal."

"Financing? Don't be silly. We're in the black and doing better every month. What's the matter, Miles? Dissatisfied with your drawing account? We could boost it."

"We wouldn't stay in the black under the new program. We need a broader capital structure."

"What new program?"

"Please, Dan. I've gone to the trouble of writing it up in detail. Let Belle read it to us."

"Well . . . okay."

Skipping the gobbledegook—like all lawyers, Miles was fond of polysyllables—Miles wanted to do three things: (a) take *Flexible Frank* away from me, hand it over to a production-engineering team, and get it on the market without delay; (b)—but I stopped it at that point. "No!"

"Wait a minute, Dan. As president and general manager, I'm certainly entitled to present my ideas in an orderly manner. Save your comments. Let Belle finish reading."

"Well . . . all right. But the answer is still 'no.'"

Point (b) was in effect that we should quit frittering around as a one-horse outfit. We had a big thing, as big as the automobile had been, and we were in at the start; therefore we should at once expand and set up organization for nationwide and worldwide selling and distribution, with production to match.

I started drumming on the table. I could just see myself as chief engineer of an outfit like that. They probably wouldn't even let me have a drafting table and if I picked up a soldering gun, the union would pull a strike. I might as well have stayed in the Army and tried to make general.

But I didn't interrupt. Point (c) was that we couldn't do this on pennies; it would take millions. Mannix Enterprises would put up the dough—what it amounted to was that we would sell out to Mannix, lock, stock, and *Flexible Frank*, and become a daughter corporation. Miles would stay on as division manager and I would stay on as chief research engineer, but the free old days would be gone; we'd both be hired hands.

"Is that all?" I said.

"Mmm . . . yes. Let's discuss it and take a vote."

"There ought to be something in there granting us the right to sit in front of the cabin at night and sing spirituals."

"This is no joke, Dan. This is how it's got to be."

"I wasn't joking. A slave needs privileges to keep him quiet. Okay, is it my turn?"

"Go ahead."

I put up a counterproposal, one that had been growing in my mind. I wanted us to get out of production. Jake Schmidt, our production shop master, was a good man; nevertheless I was forever being jerked out of a warm creative fog to straighten out bugs in production—which is like being dumped out of a warm bed into ice water. This was the real reason why I had been doing so much nightwork and staying away from the shop in the daytime. With more war-surplus buildings being moved in and a night shift contemplated I could see the time coming when I would get no peace to create, even though we turned down this utterly unpalatable plan to rub shoulders with General Motors and Consolidated. I certainly was not twins; I couldn't be both inventor and production manager.

So I proposed that we get smaller instead of bigger—license *Hired Girl* and *Window Willie*, let someone else build and sell them while we raked in the royalties. When *Flexible Frank* was ready we would license him too. If Mannix wanted the licenses and would outbid the market, swell! Meantime, we'd change our name to Davis & Gentry Research Corporation and hold it down to just the three of us, with a machinist or two to help me jackleg new gadgets. Miles and Belle could sit back and count the money as it rolled in.

Miles shook his head slowly. "No, Dan. Licensing would make us some money, granted. But not nearly the money we would make if we did it ourselves."

"Confound it, Miles, we wouldn't be doing it ourselves; that's just the point. We'd be selling our souls to the Mannix people. As for money, how much do you want? You can use only one yacht or one swimming pool at a time . . . and you'll have both before the year is out if you want them."

"I don't want them."

"What *do* you want?"

He looked up. "Dan, you want to invent things. This plan lets

41

you do so, with all the facilities and all the help and all the expense money in the world. Me, I want to run a big business. A *big* business. I've got the talent for it." He glanced at Belle. "I don't want to spend my life sitting out here in the middle of the Mojave Desert acting as business manager to one lonely inventor."

I stared at him. "You didn't talk that way at Sandia. You want out, Pappy? Belle and I would hate to see you go . . . but if that is the way you feel, I guess I could mortgage the place or something and buy you out. I wouldn't want any man to feel tied down." I was shocked to my heels, but if old Miles was restless I had no right to hold him to my pattern.

"No, I don't want out; I want us to grow. You heard my proposal. It's a formal motion for action by the corporation. I so move."

I guess I looked puzzled. "You insist on doing it the hard way? Okay, Belle, the vote is 'no.' Record it. But I won't put up my counterproposal tonight. We'll talk it over and exchange views. I want you to be happy, Miles."

Miles said stubbornly, "Let's do this properly. Roll call, Belle."

"Very well, sir. Miles Gentry, voting stock shares number——" She read off the serial numbers. "How say you?"

"Aye."

She wrote in her book.

"Daniel B. Davis, voting stock shares number——" She read off a string of telephone numbers again; I didn't listen to the formality. "How say you?"

"No. And that settles it. I'm sorry, Miles."

"Belle S. Darkin," she went on, "voting shares number——" She recited figures again. "I vote 'aye.'"

My mouth dropped open, then I managed to stop gasping and say, "But, baby, you can't do that! Those are your shares, sure, but you know perfectly well that——"

"Announce the tally," Miles growled.

"The 'ayes' have it. The proposal is carried."

"Record it."

"Yes, sir."

The next few minutes were confused. First I yelled at her, then I reasoned with her, then I snarled and told her that what she had done was not honest—true, I had assigned the stock to her but she knew as well as I did that I always voted it, that I had had no intention of parting with control of the company, that it was an engagement present, pure and simple. Hell, I had even paid the income tax on it last April. If she could pull a stunt like this when we were engaged, what was our marriage going to be like?

She looked right at me and her face was utterly strange to me. "Dan Davis, if you think we are still engaged after the way you have talked to me, you are even stupider than I've always known you were." She turned to Gentry. "Will you take me home, Miles?"

"Certainly, my dear."

I started to say something, then shut up and stalked out of there without my hat. It was high time to leave, or I would probably have killed Miles, since I couldn't touch Belle.

I didn't sleep, of course. About 4 A.M. I got out of bed, made phone calls, agreed to pay more than it was worth, and by five-thirty was in front of the plant with a pickup truck. I went to the gate, intending to unlock it and drive the truck to the loading dock so that I could run *Flexible Frank* over the tail gate—*Frank* weighed four hundred pounds.

There was a new padlock on the gate.

I shinnied over, cutting myself on barbed wire. Once inside, the gate would give me no trouble, as there were a hundred tools in the shop capable of coping with a padlock.

But the lock on the front door had been changed too.

I was looking at it, deciding whether it was easier to break a window with a tire iron, or get the jack out of the truck and brace it between the doorframe and the knob, when somebody shouted, "Hey, you! Hands up!"

I didn't put my hands up but I turned around. A middle-aged man was pointing a hogleg at me big enough to bombard a city. "Who the devil are you?"

"Who are *you?*"

"I'm Dan Davis, chief engineer of this outfit."

"Oh." He relaxed a little but still aimed the field mortar at me. "Yeah, you match the description. But if you have any identification on you, better let me see it."

"Why should I? I asked who *you* are?"

"Me? Nobody you'd know. Name of Joe Todd, with the Desert Protective & Patrol Company. Private license. You ought to know who we are; we've had you folks as clients for the night patrol for months. But tonight I'm on as special guard."

"You are? Then if they gave you a key to the place, use it. I want to get in. And quit pointing that blunderbuss at me."

He still kept it leveled at me. "I couldn't rightly do that, Mr. Davis. First place, I don't have a key. Second place, I had particular orders about you. You aren't to go in. I'll let you out the gate."

"I want the gate opened, all right, but I'm going in." I looked around for a rock to break a window.

"Please, Mr. Davis . . ."

"Huh?"

"I'd hate to see you insist, I really would. Because I couldn't chance shooting you in the legs; I ain't a very good shot. I'd have to shoot you in the belly. I've got soft-nosed bullets in this iron; it'ud be pretty messy."

I suppose that was what changed my mind, though I would like to think it was something else; i.e., when I looked again through the window I saw that *Flexible Frank* was not where I had left him.

As he let me out the gate Todd handed me an envelope. "They said to give this to you if you showed up."

I read it in the cab of the truck. It said:

18 November, 1970

Dear Mr. Davis,

At a regular meeting of the board of directors, held this date, it was voted to terminate all your connection (other than as stockholder) with the corporation, as permitted under paragraph three of your contract. It is requested that you stay off company property. Your personal papers and belongings will be forwarded to you by safe means.

The board wishes to thank you for your services and regrets the differences in policy opinion which have forced this step on us.

> *Sincerely yours,*
> *Miles Gentry*
> *Chairman of the Board and General Manager*
> *by B. S. Darkin, Sec'y-Treasurer*

I read it twice before I recalled that I had never had any contract with the corporation under which to invoke paragraph three or any other paragraph.

Later that day a bonded messenger delivered a package to the motel where I kept my clean underwear. It contained my hat, my desk pen, my other slide rule, a lot of books and personal correspondence, and a number of documents. But it did not contain my notes and drawings for *Flexible Frank*.

Some of the documents were very interesting. My "contract," for example—sure enough, paragraph three let them fire me without notice subject to three months' salary. But paragraph seven was even more interesting. It was the latest form of the yellow-dog clause, one in which the employee agrees to refrain from engaging in a competing occupation for five years by letting his former employers pay him cash to option his services on a first-refusal basis; i.e., I could go back to work any time I wanted to just by going, hat in hand, and asking Miles and Belle for a job —maybe that was why they sent the hat back.

But for five long years I could not work on household appliances without asking them first. I would rather have cut my throat.

There were copies of assignments of all patents, duly registered, from me to Hired Girl, Inc., for *Hired Girl* and *Window Willie* and a couple of minor things. (*Flexible Frank*, of course, had never been patented—well, I didn't *think* he had been patented; I found out the truth later.)

But I had never assigned any patents, I hadn't even formally licensed their use to Hired Girl, Inc.; the corporation was my own creature and there hadn't seemed to be any hurry about it.

The last three items were my stock-shares certificate (those I had not given to Belle), a certified check, and a letter explaining each item of the check—accumulated "salary" less drawing-account disbursements, three months' extra salary in lieu of notice, option money to invoke "paragraph seven" . . . and a thousand-dollar bonus to express "appreciation of services rendered." That last was real sweet of them.

While I reread that amazing collection I had time to realize that I had probably not been too bright to sign everything that Belle put in front of me. There was no possible doubt that the signatures were mine.

I steadied down enough the next day to talk it over with a lawyer, a very smart and money-hungry lawyer, one who didn't mind kicking and clapper-clawing and biting in the clinches. At first he was anxious to take it on a contingent-fee basis. But after he finished looking over my exhibits and listening to the details he sat back and laced his fingers over his belly and looked sour. "Dan, I'm going to give you some advice and it's not going to cost you anything."

"Well?"

"Do nothing. You haven't got a prayer."

"But you said——"

"I know what I said. They rooked you. But how can you prove it? They were too smart to steal your stock or cut you off without a penny. They gave you exactly the deal you could have reasonably expected if everything had been kosher and you had quit, or had been fired over—as they express it—a difference of policy opinion. They gave you everything you had coming to you . . . and a measly thousand to boot, just to show there are no hard feelings."

"But I didn't *have* a contract! And I *never* assigned those patents!"

"These papers say you did. You admit that's your signature. Can you prove what you say by anyone else?"

I thought about it. I certainly could not. Not even Jake Schmidt knew anything that went on in the front office. The only witnesses I had were . . . Miles and Belle.

"Now about that stock assignment," he went on, "that's the one chance to break the log jam. If you——"

"But that is the only transaction in the whole stack that really *is* legitimate. I signed over that stock to her."

"Yes, but why? You say that you gave it to her as an engagement present in expectation of marriage. Never mind how she voted it; that's beside the point. If you can prove that it was given as a betrothal gift in full expectation of marriage, and that she knew it when she accepted it, you can force her either to marry you or to disgorge. McNulty *vs.* Rhodes. Then you're in control again and you kick them out. Can you prove it?"

"Damn it, I don't want to marry her now. I wouldn't have her."

"That's your problem. But one thing at a time. Have you any

46

witnesses or any evidence, letters or anything, which would tend to show that she accepted it, understanding that you were giving it to her as your future wife?"

I thought. Sure, I had witnesses . . . the same old two, Miles and Belle.

"You see? With nothing but your word against both of theirs, plus a pile of written evidence, you not only won't get anywhere, but you might wind up committed to a Napoleon factory with a diagnosis of paranoia. My advice to you is to get a job in some other line . . . or at the very most go ahead and buck their yellow-dog contract by setting up a competitive business—I'd like to see that phraseology tested, as long as I didn't have to fight it myself. But don't charge them with conspiracy. They'll win, then they'll sue you and clean you out of what they let you keep." He stood up.

I took only part of his advice. There was a bar on the ground floor of the same building; I went in and had a couple or nine drinks.

I had plenty of time to recall all this while I was driving out to see Miles. Once we had started making money, he had moved Ricky and himself to a nice little rental in San Fernando Valley to get out of the murderous Mojave heat and had started commuting via the Air Force Slot. Ricky wasn't there now, I was happy to recall; she was up at Big Bear Lake at Girl Scout camp —I didn't want to chance Ricky's being witness to a row between me and her stepdaddy.

I was bumper to bumper in Sepulveda Tunnel when it occurred to me that it would be smart to get the certificate for my Hired Girl stock off my person before going to see Miles. I did not expect any rough stuff (unless I started it), but it just seemed a good idea . . . like a cat who has had his tail caught in the screen door once, I was permanently suspicious.

Leave it in the car? Suppose I was hauled in for assault and battery; it wouldn't be smart to have it in the car when the car was towed in and impounded.

I could mail it to myself, but I had been getting my mail lately from general delivery at the G.P.O., while shifting from hotel to hotel as often as they found out I was keeping a cat.

I had better mail it to someone I could trust.

But that was a mighty short list.

Then I remembered someone I *could* trust.

Ricky.

I may seem a glutton for punishment to decide to trust one female just after I had been clipped by another. But the cases are not parallel. I had known Ricky half her life and if there ever was a human being honest as a Jo block, Ricky was she . . . and Pete thought so too. Besides, Ricky didn't have physical specifications capable of warping a man's judgment. Her femininity was only in her face; it hadn't affected her figure yet.

When I managed to escape from the log jam in Sepulveda Tunnel I got off the throughway and found a drugstore; there I bought stamps and a big and a little envelope and some note paper. I wrote to her:

Dear Rikki-tikki-tavi,

I hope to see you soon but until I do, I want you to keep this inside envelope for me. It's a secret, just between you and me.

I stopped and thought. Doggone it, if anything happened to me . . . oh, even a car crash, or anything that can stop breathing . . . while Ricky had this, eventually it would wind up with Miles and Belle. Unless I rigged things to prevent it. I realized as I thought about it that I had subconsciously reached a decision about the cold-sleep deal; I wasn't going to take it. Sobering up and the lecture the doc had read me had stiffened my spine; I wasn't going to run away, I was going to stay and fight—and this stock certificate was my best weapon. It gave me the right to examine the books; it entitled me to poke my nose into any and all affairs of the company. If they tried again simply to keep me out with a hired guard I could go back next time with a lawyer and a deputy sheriff and a court order.

I could drag them into court with it too. Maybe I couldn't win but I could make a stink and perhaps cause the Mannix people to shy off from buying them out.

Maybe I shouldn't send it to Ricky at all.

No, if anything happened to me I wanted her to have it. Ricky and Pete were all the "family" I had. I went on writing:

If by any chance I don't see you for a year, you'll know some-thing has happened to me. If that happens, take care of Pete, if you can find him—and without telling anybody take the inside envelope to a branch of the Bank of America, give it to the trust officer and tell him to open it.

Love and kisses,
Uncle Danny

Then I took another sheet and wrote: "3 December, 1970, Los Angeles, California— For one dollar in hand received and other valuable considerations I assign"—here I listed legal descriptions and serial numbers of my Hired Girl, Inc., stock shares—"to the Bank of America in trust for Frederica Virginia Gentry and to be reassigned to her on her twenty-first birthday," and signed it. The intent was clear and it was the best I could do on a drugstore counter with a juke box blaring in my ear. It should make sure that Ricky got the stock if anything happened to me, while mak-ing darn sure that Miles and Belle could not grab it away from her.

But if all went well, I would just ask Ricky to give the enve-lope back to me when I got around to it. By not using the assign-ment form printed on the back of the certificate, I avoided all the red tape of having a minor assign it back to me; I could just tear up the separate sheet of paper.

I sealed the stock certificate with the note assigning it into the smaller envelope, placed it and the letter to Ricky in the larger envelope, addressed it to Ricky at the Girl Scout camp, stamped it, and dropped it in the box outside the drugstore. I noted that it would be picked up in about forty minutes and climbed back into my car feeling positively lighthearted . . . not because I had safe-guarded the stock but because I had solved my greater problems.

Well, not "solved" them, perhaps, but had decided to face them, not run off and crawl in a hole to play Rip van Winkle . . . nor try to blot them out again with ethanol in various flavors. Sure, I wanted to see the year 2000, but just by sitting tight I *would* see it . . . when I was sixty, and still young enough, probably, to whistle at the girls. No hurry. Jumping to the next century in one long nap wouldn't be satisfactory to a normal man anyhow —about like seeing the end of a movie without having seen what goes before. The thing to do with the next thirty years was to enjoy them while they unfolded; then when I came to the year 2000 I would understand it.

In the meantime I was going to have one lulu of a fight with Miles and Belle. Maybe I wouldn't win, but I would sure let them know they had been in a scrap—like the times Pete had come home bleeding in six directions but insisting loudly, "You ought to see the other cat!"

I didn't expect much out of this interview tonight. All it would amount to was a formal declaration of war. I planned to ruin Miles's sleep . . . and he could phone Belle and ruin hers.

III

By the time I got to Miles's house I was whistling. I had quit worrying about that precious pair and had worked out in my head, in the last fifteen miles, two brand-new gadgets, either one of which could make me rich. One was a drafting machine, to be operated like an electric typewriter. I guessed that there must be easily fifty thousand engineers in the U.S. alone bending over drafting boards every day and hating it, because it gets you in your kidneys and ruins your eyes. Not that they didn't want to design—they did want to—but physically it was much too hard work.

This gismo would let them sit down in a big easy chair and tap keys and have the picture unfold on an easel above the keyboard. Depress three keys simultaneously and have a horizontal line appear just where you want it; depress another key and you fillet it in with a vertical line; depress two keys and then two more in succession and draw a line at an exact slant.

Cripes, for a small additional cost as an accessory, I could add a second easel, let an architect design in isometric (the only easy way to design), and have the second picture come out in perfect perspective rendering without his even looking at it. Why, I could even set the thing to pull floor plans and elevations right out of the isometric.

The beauty of it was that it could be made almost entirely with standard parts, most of them available at radio shops and camera stores. All but the control board, that is, and I was sure I could bread-board a rig for that by buying an electric typewriter, tearing its guts out, and hooking the keys to operate these other circuits. A month to make a primitive model, six weeks more to chase bugs . . .

But that one I just tucked away in the back of my mind, certain that I could do it and that it would have a market. The thing that really delighted me was that I had figured out a way to outflex poor old *Flexible Frank*. I knew more about *Frank* than anyone else could learn, even if they studied him a year. What they could not know, what even my notes did not show, was that there was at least one workable alternative for every choice I had made— and that my choices had been constrained by thinking of him as a household servant. To start with, I could throw away the restriction that he had to live in a powered wheel chair. From there on I could do anything, except that I would need the Thorsen memory tubes—and Miles could not keep me from using those; they were on the market for anyone who wanted to design a cybernetic sequence.

The drafting machine could wait; I'd get busy on the unlimited all-purpose automaton, capable of being programmed for *anything* a man could do, just as long as it did not require true human judgment.

No, I'd rig a drafting machine first, then use it to design *Protean Pete*. "How about that, Pete? We're going to name the world's first real robot after you."

"Mrrrrarr?"

"Don't be so suspicious; it's an honor." After breaking in on *Frank*, I could design Pete right at my drafting machine, really refine it, and quickly. I'd make it a killer, a triple-threat demon that would displace *Frank* before they ever got him into production. With any luck I'd run them broke and have them begging me to come back. Kill the goose that lays the golden eggs, would they?

There were lights on in Miles's house and his car was at the curb. I parked in front of Miles's car, said to Pete, "You'd better stay here, fellow, and protect the car. Holler 'halt' three times fast, then shoot to kill."

"Nooo!"

"If you go inside you'll have to stay in the bag."

"Bleerrrt?"

"Don't argue. If you want to come in, get in your bag."

Pete jumped into the bag.

Miles let me in. Neither of us offered to shake hands. He led me into his living room and gestured at a chair.

Belle was there. I had not expected her, but I suppose it was not surprising. I looked at her and grinned. "Fancy meeting you here! Don't tell me you came all the way from Mojave just to talk to little old me?" Oh, I'm a gallus-snapper when I get started; you should see me wear women's hats at parties.

Belle frowned. "Don't be funny, Dan. Say what you have to say, if anything, and get out."

"Don't hurry me. I think this is cozy . . . my former partner . . . my former fiancée. All we lack is my former business."

Miles said placatingly, "Now, Dan, don't take that attitude. We did it for your own good . . . and you can come back to work any time you want to. I'd be glad to have you back."

"For my own good, eh? That sounds like what they told the horse thief when they hanged him. As for coming back—how about it, Belle? Can I come back?"

She bit her lip. "If Miles says so, of course."

"It seems like only yesterday that it used to be: 'If Dan says so, of course.' But everything changes; that's life. And I'm not coming back, kids; you can stop fretting. I just came here tonight to find out some things."

Miles glanced at Belle. She answered, "Such as?"

"Well, first, which one of you cooked up the swindle? Or did you plan it together?"

Miles said slowly, "That's an ugly word, Dan. I don't like it."

"Oh, come, come, let's not be mealymouthed. If the word is ugly, the deed is ten times as ugly. I mean faking a yellow-dog contract, faking patent assignments—that one is a federal offense, Miles; I think they pipe sunlight to you on alternate Wednesdays. I'm not sure, but no doubt the FBI can tell me. Tomorrow," I added, seeing him flinch.

"Dan, you're not going to be silly enough to try to make trouble about this?"

"Trouble? I'm going to hit you in all directions, civil and criminal, on all counts. You'll be too busy to scratch . . . unless you agree to do one thing. But I didn't mention your third peccadillo —theft of my notes and drawings of *Flexible Frank* . . . and the working model, too, although you may be able to make me pay for the materials for that, since I did bill them to the company."

"Theft, nonsense!" snapped Belle. "You were working for the company."

"Was I? I did most of it at night. And I never was an employee, Belle, as you both know. I simply drew living expenses against profits earned by my shares. What is the Mannix outfit going to say when I file a criminal complaint, charging that the things they were interested in buying—*Hired Girl, Willie,* and *Frank* —never did belong to the company but were stolen from me?"

"Nonsense," Belle repeated grimly. "You were working for the company. You had a contract."

I leaned back and laughed. "Look, kids, you don't have to lie now; save it for the witness stand. There ain't nobody here but just us chickens. What I really want to know is this: who thought it up? I know how it was done. Belle, you used to bring in papers for me to sign. If more than one copy had to be signed, you would paper-clip the other copies to the first—for my convenience, of course; you were always the perfect secretary—and all I would see of the copies underneath would be the place to sign my name. Now I know that you slipped some jokers into some of those neat piles. So I know that you were the one who conducted the mechanics of the swindle; Miles could not have done it. Shucks, Miles can't even type very well. But who worded those documents you horsed me into signing? You? I don't think so . . . unless you've had legal training you never mentioned. How about it, Miles? Could a mere stenographer phrase that wonderful clause seven so perfectly? Or did it take a lawyer? *You,* I mean."

Miles's cigar had long since gone out. He took it from his mouth, looked at it, and said carefully, "Dan, old friend, if you think you'll trap us into admissions, you're crazy."

"Oh, come off it; we're alone. You're both guilty either way. But I'd like to think that Delilah over there came to you with the whole thing wrapped up, complete, and then tempted you into a moment of weakness. But I know it's not true. Unless Belle is a lawyer herself, you were both in it, accomplices before and after. You wrote the double talk; she typed it and tricked me into signing. Right?"

"Don't answer, Miles!"

"Of course I won't answer," Miles agreed. "He may have a recorder hidden in that bag."

"I should have had," I agreed, "but I don't." I spread the top of the bag and Pete stuck his head out. "You getting it all, Pete? Careful what you say, folks; Pete has an elephant's memory. No, I didn't bring a recorder—I'm just good old lunkheaded Dan Davis who never thinks ahead. I go stumbling along, trusting my friends . . . the way I trusted you two. Is Belle a lawyer, Dan? Or did you yourself sit down in cold blood and plan how you could hog-tie me and rob me and make it look legal?"

"Dan!" interrupted Belle. "With his skill, he could make a recorder the size of a pack of cigarettes. It may not be in the bag. It may be on him."

"That's a good idea, Belle. Next time I'll have one."

"I'm aware of that, my dear," Miles answered. "If he has, you are talking very loosely. Mind your tongue."

Belle answered with a word I didn't know she used. My eyebrows went up. "Snapping at each other? Trouble between thieves already?"

Miles's temper was stretching thin, I was happy to see. He answered, "Mind *your* tongue, Dan . . . if you want to stay healthy."

"Tsk, tsk! I'm younger than you are and I've had the judo course a lot more recently. And you wouldn't shoot a man; you'd frame him with some sort of fake legal document. 'Thieves,' I said, and 'thieves' I meant. Thieves and liars, both of you." I turned to Belle. "My old man taught me never to call a lady a liar, sugar face, but you aren't a lady. You're a liar . . . and a thief . . . and a tramp."

Belle turned red and gave me a look in which all her beauty vanished and the underlying predatory animal was all that remained. "Miles!" she said shrilly. "Are you going to sit there and let him——"

"Quiet!" Miles ordered. "His rudeness is calculated. It's intended to make us get excited and say things we'll regret. Which you are almost doing. So keep quiet." Belle shut up, but her face was still feral. Miles turned to me. "Dan, I'm a practical man always, I hope. I tried to make you see reason before you walked out of the firm. In the settlement I tried to make it such that you would take the inevitable gracefully."

"Be raped quietly, you mean."

"As you will. I still want a peaceful settlement. You couldn't win any sort of suit, but as a lawyer I know that it is always better to stay out of court than to win. If possible. You mentioned a while ago that there was some one thing I could do that would placate you. Tell me what it is; perhaps we can reach terms."

"Oh, that. I was coming to it. *You* can't do it, but perhaps you can arrange it. It's simple. Get Belle to assign back to me the stock I assigned to her as an engagement present."

"No!" said Belle.

Miles said, "I told you to keep quiet."

I looked at her and said, "Why not, my former dear? I've taken advice on this point, as the lawyers put it, and, since it was given in consideration of the fact that you promised to marry me, you are not only morally but legally bound to return it. It was not a 'free gift,' as I believe the expression is, but something handed over for an expected and contracted consideration which I never received, to wit, your somewhat lovely self. So how about coughing up, huh? Or have you changed your mind again and are now willing to marry me?"

She told me where and how I could expect to marry her.

Miles said tiredly, "Belle, you're only making things worse. Don't you understand that he is trying to get our goats?" He turned back to me. "Dan, if that is what you came over for, you may as well leave. I stipulate that if the circumstances had been as you alleged, you might have a point. But they were not. You transferred that stock to Belle for value received."

"Huh? What value? Where's the canceled check?"

"There didn't need be any. For services to the company beyond her duties."

I stared. "What a lovely theory! Look, Miles old boy, if it was for service to the company and not to me personally, then you must have known about it and would have been anxious to pay her the same amount—after all, we split the profits fifty-fifty even if I had . . . or thought I had . . . retained control. Don't tell me you gave Belle a block of stock of the same size?"

Then I saw them glance at each other and I got a wild hunch. "Maybe you did! I'll bet my little dumpling made you do it, or she wouldn't play. Is that right? If so, you can bet your life she registered the transfer at once . . . and the dates will show that *I* transferred stock to her at the very time we got engaged—shucks, the engagement was in the *Desert Herald*—while *you* transferred stock to her when you put the skids under me and she jilted me— and it's all a matter of record! Maybe a judge *will* believe me, Miles? What do you think?"

I had cracked them, I had cracked them! I could tell from the way their faces went blank that I had stumbled on the one circumstance they could never explain and one I was never meant to know. So I crowded them . . . and had another wild guess. Wild? No, logical. "How much stock, Belle? As much as you got out of me, just for being 'engaged'? You did more for him; you should have gotten more." I stopped suddenly. "Say . . . I thought it was odd that Belle came all the way over here just to talk to me, seeing how she hates that trip. Maybe you didn't come all that way; maybe you were here all along. Are you two shacked up? Or should I say 'engaged'? Or . . . are you already married?" I thought about it. "I'll bet you are. Miles, you aren't as starry-eyed as I am; I'll bet my other shirt that you would never, never transfer stock to Belle simply on promise of marriage. But you might for a wedding present—provided you got back voting control of it. Don't bother to answer; tomorrow I'm going to start digging for the facts. They'll be on record too."

Miles glanced at Belle and said, "Don't waste your time. Meet Mrs. Gentry."

"So? Congratulations, both of you. You deserve each other. Now about my stock. Since Mrs. Gentry obviously can't marry me, then——"

"Don't be silly, Dan. I've already offset your ridiculous theory. I did make a stock transfer to Belle just as you did. For the same reason, services to the firm. As you say, these things are matters of record. Belle and I were married just a week ago . . . but you

57

will find the stock registered to her quite some time ago if you care to look it up. You can't connect them. No, she received stock from both of us, because of her great value to the firm. Then after you jilted her and after you left the employ of the firm, we were married."

It set me back. Miles was too smart to tell a lie I could check on so easily. But there was something about it that was not true, something more than I had as yet found out.

"When and where were you married?"

"Santa Barbara courthouse, last Thursday. Not that it is your business."

"Perhaps not. When was the stock transfer?"

"I don't know exactly. Look it up if you want to know."

Damn it, it just did not ring true that he had handed stock over to Belle before he had her committed to him. That was the sort of sloppy stunt I pulled; it wasn't in character for him. "I'm wondering something, Miles. If I put a detective to work on it, might I find that the two of you got married once before a little earlier than that? Maybe in Yuma? Or Las Vegas? Or maybe you ducked over to Reno that time you both went north for the tax hearings? Maybe it would turn out that there was such a marriage recorded, and maybe the date of the stock transfer and the dates my patents were assigned to the firm all made a pretty pattern. Huh?"

Miles did not crack; he did not even look at Belle. As for Belle, the hate in her face could not have been increased even by a lucky stab in the dark. Yet it seemed to fit and I decided to ride the hunch to the limit.

Miles simply said, "Dan, I've been patient with you and have tried to be conciliatory. All it's got me is abuse. So I think it's time you left. Or I'll bloody well make a stab at throwing you out—you and your flea-bitten cat!"

"Olé!" I answered. "That's the first manly thing you've said tonight. But don't call Pete 'flea-bitten.' He understands English and he is likely to take a chunk out of you. Okay, ex-pal, I'll get out . . . but I want to make a short curtain speech, very short. It's probably the last word I'll ever have to say to you. Okay?"

"Well . . . okay. Make it short."

Belle said urgently, "Miles, I want to talk to you."

He motioned her to be quiet without looking at her. "Go ahead. Be brief."

I turned to Belle. "You probably won't want to hear this, Belle. I suggest that you leave."

She stayed, of course. I wanted to be sure she would. I looked back at him. "Miles, I'm not too angry with you. The things a man will do for a larcenous woman are beyond belief. If Samson and Mark Antony were vulnerable, why should I expect you to be immune? By rights, instead of being angry I should be grateful to you. I guess I am, a little. I do know I'm sorry for you." I looked over at Belle. "You've got her now and she's all your problem . . . and all it has cost me is a little money and temporarily my peace of mind. But what will she cost *you*? She cheated me, she even managed to persuade you, my trusted friend, to cheat me . . . what day will she team up with a new cat's-paw and start cheating you? Next week? Next month? As long as next year? As surely as a dog returns to its vomit——"

"Miles!" Belle shrilled.

Miles said dangerously, "Get out!" and I knew he meant it. So I stood up.

"We were just going. I'm sorry for you, old fellow. Both of us made just one mistake originally, and it was as much my fault as yours. But you've got to pay for it alone. And that's too bad . . . because it was such an innocent mistake."

His curiosity got him. "What do you mean?"

"We should have wondered why a woman so smart and beautiful and competent and all-around high-powered was willing to come to work for us at clerk-typist's wages. If we had taken her fingerprints the way the big firms do, and run a routine check, we might not have hired her . . . and you and I would still be partners."

Pay dirt again! Miles looked suddenly at his wife and she looked —well, "cornered rat" is wrong; rats aren't shaped like Belle.

And I couldn't leave well enough alone; I just had to pick at it. I walked toward her, saying, "Well, Belle? If I took that highball glass sitting beside you and had the fingerprints on it checked, what would I find? Pictures in post offices? The big con? Or bigamy? Marrying suckers for their money, maybe? Is Miles legally your husband?" I reached down and picked up the glass.

Belle slapped it out of my hand.

And Miles shouted at me.

And I had finally pushed my luck too far. I had been stupid to go into a cage of dangerous animals with no weapons, then I forgot the first tenet of the animal tamer; I turned my back. Miles shouted and I turned toward him. Belle reached for her purse . . . and I remember thinking that it was a hell of a time for her to be reaching for a cigarette.

Then I felt the stab of the needle.

I remember feeling just one thing as my knees got weak and I started slipping toward the carpet: utter astonishment that Belle would do such a thing to me. When it came right down to it, I still trusted her.

IV

I never was completely unconscious. I got dizzy and vague as the drug hit me—it hits even quicker than morphine. But that was all. Miles yelled something at Belle and grabbed me around the chest as my knees folded. As he dragged me over and let me collapse into a chair, even the dizziness passed.

But while I was awake, part of me was dead. I know now what they used on me: the "zombie" drug, Uncle Sam's answer to brainwashing. So far as I know, we never used it on a prisoner, but the boys whipped it up in the investigation of brainwashing and there it was, illegal but very effective. It's the same stuff they now use in one-day psychoanalysis, but I believe it takes a court order to permit even a psychiatrist to use it.

God knows where Belle laid hands on it. But then God alone knows what other suckers she had on the string.

But I wasn't wondering about that then; I wasn't wondering about anything. I just lay slumped there, passive as a vegetable, hearing what went on, seeing anything in front of my eyes—but if Lady Godiva had strolled through without her horse I would not have shifted my eyes as she passed out of my vision.

Unless I was told to.

Pete jumped out of his bag, trotted over to where I slouched, and asked what was wrong. When I didn't answer he started stropping my shins vigorously back and forth while still demanding an explanation. When still I did not respond he levitated to my knees, put his forepaws on my chest, looked me right in the face, and demanded to know what was wrong, right now and no nonsense.

I didn't answer and he began to wail.

That caused Miles and Belle to pay attention to him. Once Miles had me in the chair he had turned to Belle and had said bitterly, "Now you've done it! Have you gone crazy?"

Belle answered, "Keep your nerve, Chubby. We're going to settle him once and for all."

"What? If you think I'm going to help in a *murder*——"

"Stuff it! That would be the logical thing to do . . . but you don't have the guts for it. Fortunately it's not necessary with that stuff in him."

"What do you mean?"

"He's our boy now. He'll do what I tell him to. He won't make any more trouble."

"But . . . good God, Belle, you can't keep him doped up forever. Once he comes out of it——"

"Quit talking like a lawyer. I know what this stuff will do; you don't. When he comes out of it he'll do whatever I've told him to do. I'll tell him never to sue us; he'll never sue us. I tell him to quit sticking his nose into our business; okay, he'll leave us alone. I tell him to go to Timbuktu; he'll go there. I tell him to forget all this; he'll forget . . . but he'll do it just the same."

I listened, understanding her but not in the least interested. If somebody had shouted, "The house is on fire!" I would have understood that, too, and I still would not have been interested.

"I don't believe it."

"You don't, eh?" She looked at him oddly. "You ought to."

"Huh? What do you mean?"

"Skip it, skip it. This stuff works, Chubby. But first we've got to——"

It was then that Pete started wailing. You don't hear a cat wail very often; you could go a lifetime and not hear it. They don't do it when fighting, no matter how badly they are hurt; they never do it out of simple displeasure. A cat does it only in ultimate distress, when the situation is utterly unbearable but beyond its capacity and there is nothing left to do but keen.

It puts one in mind of a banshee. Also it is hardly to be endured; it hits a nerve-racking frequency.

Miles turned and said, "That confounded cat! We've got to get it out of here."

Belle said, "Kill it."

"Huh? You're always too drastic, Belle. Why, Dan would raise more Cain about that worthless animal than he would if we had stripped him completely. Here——" He turned and picked up Pete's travel bag.

"*I'll* kill it!" Belle said savagely. "I've wanted to kill that damned cat for months." She looked around for a weapon and found one, a poker from the fireplace set; she ran over and grabbed it.

Miles picked up Pete and tried to put him into the bag.

"Tried" is the word. Pete isn't anxious to be picked up by anyone but me or Ricky, and even I would not pick him up while he was wailing, without very careful negotiation; an emotionally disturbed cat is as touchy as mercury fulminate. But even if he were not upset, Pete certainly would never permit himself without protest to be picked up by the scruff of the neck.

Pete got him with claws in the forearm and teeth in the fleshy part of Miles's left thumb. Miles yelped and dropped him.

Belle shrilled, "Stand clear, Chubby!" and swung at him with the poker.

Belle's intentions were sufficiently forthright and she had the strength and the weapon. But she wasn't skilled with her weapon, whereas Pete is very skilled with his. He ducked under that roundhouse swipe and hit her four ways, two paws for each of her legs.

Belle screamed and dropped the poker.

I didn't see much of the rest of it. I was still looking straight ahead and could see most of the living room, but I couldn't see anything outside that angle because no one told me to look in any other direction. So I followed the rest of it mostly by sound, except once when they doubled back across my cone of vision, two people chasing a cat—then with unbelievable suddenness, two people being chased by a cat. Aside from that one short scene I was aware of the battle by the sounds of crashes, running, shouts, curses, and screams.

63

But I don't think they ever laid a glove on him.

The worst thing that happened to me that night was that in Pete's finest hour, his greatest battle and greatest victory, I not only did not see all the details, but I was totally unable to appreciate any of it. I saw and I heard but I had no feeling about it; at his supreme Moment of Truth I was numb.

I recall it now and conjure up emotion I could not feel then. But it's not the same thing; I'm forever deprived, like a narcolept on a honeymoon.

The crashes and curses ceased abruptly, and shortly Miles and Belle came back into the living room. Belle said between gasps, "Who left that censorable screen door unhooked?"

"You did. Shut up about it. It's gone now." Miles had blood on his face as well as his hands; he dabbed at the fresh scratches on his face and did them no good. At some point he must have tripped and gone down, for his clothes looked it and his coat was split up the back.

"I will like hell shut up. Have you got a gun in the house?"

"Huh?"

"I'm going to shoot that damned cat." Belle was in even worse shape than Miles; she had more skin where Pete could get at it—legs, bare arms and shoulders. It was clear that she would not be wearing strapless dresses again soon, and unless she got expert attention promptly she was likely to have scars. She looked like a harpy after a no-holds-barred row with her sisters.

Miles said, "Sit down!"

She answered him briefly and, by implication, negatively. "I'm going to kill that cat."

"Then don't sit down. Go wash yourself. I'll help you with iodine and stuff and you can help me. But forget that cat; we're well rid of it."

Belle answered rather incoherently, but Miles understood her. "You too," he answered, "in spades. Look here, Belle, if I did have a gun—I'm not saying that I have—and you went out there and started shooting, whether you got the cat or not you would have the police here inside of ten minutes, snooping around and asking questions. Do you want *that* with *him* on our hands?" He jerked a thumb in my direction. "And if you go outside the house tonight without a gun that beast will probably kill you." He scowled even more deeply. "There ought to be a law against keeping an animal like that. He's a public danger. Listen to him."

We could all hear Pete prowling around the house. He was not wailing now; he was voicing his war cry—inviting them to choose weapons and come outside, singly or in bunches.

Belle listened to it and shuddered. Miles said, "Don't worry; he can't get in. I not only hooked the screen you left open, I locked the door."

"I did not leave it open!"

"Have it your own way." Miles went around checking the window fastenings. Presently Belle left the room and so did he. Sometime while they were gone Pete shut up. I don't know how long they were gone; time didn't mean anything to me.

Belle came back first. Her make-up and hairdo were perfect; she had put on a long-sleeved, high-necked dress and had replaced the ruined stockings. Except for Band-Aid strips on her face, the results of battle did not show. Had it not been for the grim look on her phiz I would have considered her, under other circumstances, a delectable sight.

She came straight toward me and told me to stand up, so I did. She went through me quickly and expertly, not forgetting watch pocket, shirt pockets, and the diagonal one on the left inside of the jacket which most suits do not have. The take was not much— my wallet with a small amount of cash, ID cards, driver's license, and such, keys, small change, a nasal inhaler against the smog, minor miscellaneous junk, and the envelope containing the certified check which she herself had bought and had sent to me. She turned it over, read the closed endorsement I had made on it, and looked puzzled.

"What's this, Dan? Buying a slug of insurance?"

"No." I would have told her the rest, but answering the last question asked of me was the best I could do.

She frowned and put it with the rest of the contents of my pockets. Then she caught sight of Pete's bag and apparently recalled the flap in it I used for a brief case, for she picked it up and opened the flap.

At once she found the quadruplicate sets of the dozen and a half forms I had signed for Mutual Assurance Company. She sat down and started to read them. I stood where she had left me, a tailor's dummy waiting to be put away.

Presently Miles came in wearing bathrobe and slippers and quite a large amount of gauze and adhesive tape. He looked like a fourth-rate middleweight whose manager has let him be out-matched. He was wearing one bandage like a scalp lock, fore and aft on his bald head; Pete must have got to him while he was down.

Belle glanced up, waved him to silence, and indicated the stack of papers she was through with. He sat down and started to read. He caught up with her and finished the last one reading over her shoulder.

She said, "This puts a different complexion on things."

"An understatement. This commitment order is for December fourth—that's *tomorrow*. Belle, he's as hot as noon in Mojave; we've got to get him out of here!" He glanced at a clock. "They'll be looking for him in the morning."

"Miles, you always get chicken when the pressure is on. This is a break, maybe the best break we could hope for."

"How do you figure?"

"This zombie soup, good as it is, has one shortcoming. Suppose you dose somebody with it and load him up with what you want him to do. Okay, so he does it. He carries out your orders; he has to. Know anything about hypnosis?"

"Not much."

"Do you know *anything* but law, Chubby? You haven't any curiosity. A posthypnotic command—which is what this amounts to—may conflict, in fact it's almost certain to conflict, with what the subject really wants to do. Eventually that may land him in the hands of a psychiatrist. If the psychiatrist is any good, he's likely to find out what the trouble is. It is just possible that Dan here might go to one and get unstuck from whatever orders I give him. If he did, he could make plenty of trouble."

"Damn it, you told me this drug was sure-fire."

"Good God, Chubby, you have to take chances with everything in life. That's what makes it fun. Let me think."

After a bit she said, "The simplest thing and the safest is to let him go ahead with this sleep jump he is all set to take. He wouldn't be any more out of our hair if he was dead—and we don't

66

have to take any risk. Instead of having to give him a bunch of complicated orders and then praying that he won't come unstuck, all we have to do is order him to go ahead with the cold sleep, then sober him up and get him out of here . . . or get him out of here and then sober him." She turned to me. "Dan, when are you going to take the Sleep?"

"I'm not."

"Huh? What's all this?" She gestured at the papers from my bag.

"Papers for cold sleep. Contracts with Mutual Assurance."

"He's nutty," Miles commented.

"Mmm . . . of course he is. I keep forgetting that they can't really think when they're under it. They can hear and talk and answer questions . . . but it has to be just the right questions. They can't think." She came up close and looked me in the eyes. "Dan, I want you to tell me all about this cold-sleep deal. Start at the beginning and tell it all the way through. You've got all the papers here to do it; apparently you signed them just today. Now you say you aren't going to do it. Tell me all about it, because I want to know why you were going to do it and now you say you aren't."

So I told her. Put that way, I could answer. It took a long time to tell as I did just what she said and told it all the way through in detail.

"So you sat there in that drive-in and decided not to? You decided to come out here and make trouble for us instead?"

"Yes." I was about to go on, tell about the trip out, tell her what I had said to Pete and what he had said to me, tell her how I had stopped at a drugstore and taken care of my Hired Girl stock, how I had driven then to Miles's house, how Pete had not wanted to wait in the car, how——

But she did not give me a chance. She said, "You've changed your mind again, Dan. You *want* to take the cold sleep. You're going to take the cold sleep. You won't let anything in the world stand in the way of your taking the cold sleep. Understand me? What are you going to do?"

"I'm going to take the cold sleep. I want to take . . ." I started to sway. I had been standing like a flagpole for more than an hour,

I would guess, without moving any muscle, because no one had told me to. I started collapsing slowly toward her.

She jumped back and said sharply, "Sit down!"

So I sat down.

Belle turned to Miles. "That does it. I'll hammer away at it until I'm sure he can't miss."

Miles looked at the clock. "He said that doctor wanted him there at noon."

"Plenty of time. But we had better drive him there ourselves, just to be—— No, damn it!"

"What's the trouble?"

"The time *is* too short. I gave him enough soup for a horse, because I wanted it to hit him fast—before he hit me. By noon he'd be sober enough to convince most people. But not a doctor."

"Maybe it'll just be perfunctory. His physical examination is already here and signed."

"You heard what he said the doctor told him. The doctor's going to check him to see if he's had anything to drink. That means he'll test his reflexes and take his reaction time and peer in his eyes and—oh, all the things we don't want done. The things we don't dare let a doctor do. Miles, it won't work."

"How about the next day? Call 'em up and tell them there has been a slight delay?"

"Shut up and let me think."

Presently she started looking over the papers I had brought with me. Then she left the room, returned immediately with a jeweler's loop, which she screwed into her right eye like a monocle, and proceeded to examine each paper with great care. Miles asked her what she was doing, but she brushed his question aside.

Presently she took the loop out of her eye and said, "Thank goodness they all have to use the same government forms. Chubby, get me the yellow-pages phone book."

"What for?"

"Get it, get it. I want to check the exact phrasing of a firm name—oh, I know what it is but I want to be sure."

Grumbling, Miles fetched it. She thumbed through it, then said, "Yes, 'Master Insurance Company of California' . . . and there's room enough on each of them. I wish it could be 'Motors' instead of 'Master'; that would be a cinch—but I don't have any connections at 'Motors Insurance,' and besides, I'm not sure they even handle hibernation; I think they're just autos and trucks." She looked up. "Chubby, you're going to have to drive me out to the plant right away."

"Huh?"

"Unless you know of some quicker way to get an electric typewriter with executive type face and carbon ribbon. No, you go out by yourself and fetch it back; I've got telephoning to do."

He frowned. "I'm beginning to see what you plan to do. But, Belle, this is crazy. This is fantastically dangerous."

She laughed. "That's what you think. I told you I had good connections before we ever teamed up. Could you have swung the Mannix deal alone?"

"Well . . . I don't know."

"*I* know. And maybe you don't know that Master Insurance is part of the Mannix group."

"Well, no, I didn't. And I don't see what difference it makes."

"It means my connections are still good. See here, Chubby, the firm I used to work for used to help Mannix Enterprises with their tax losses . . . until my boss left the country. How do you think we got such a good deal without being able to guarantee that Danny boy went with the deal? I know all about Mannix. Now hurry up and get that typewriter and I'll let you watch an artist at work. Watch out for that cat."

Miles grumbled but started to leave, then returned. "Belle? Didn't Dan park right in front of the house?"

"Why?"

"His car isn't there now." He looked worried.

"Well, he probably parked around the corner. It's unimportant. Go get that typewriter. Hurry!"

He left again. I could have told them where I had parked but, since they did not ask me, I did not think about it. I did not think at all.

Belle went elsewhere in the house and left me alone. Sometime around daylight Miles got back, looking haggard and carrying our heavy typewriter. Then I was left alone again.

Once Belle came back in and said, "Dan, you've got a paper there telling the insurance company to take care of your Hired Girl stock. You don't want to do that; you want to give it to me."

I didn't answer. She looked annoyed and said, "Let's put it this way. You do want to give it to me. You know you want to give it to me. You know that, don't you?"

"Yes. I want to give it to you."

"Good. You want to give it to me. You have to give it to me. You won't be happy until you do give it to me. Now where is it? Is it in your car?"

"No."

"Then where is it?"

"I mailed it."

"*What?*" She grew shrill. "When did you mail it? Who did you mail it to? Why did you do it?"

If she had asked the second question last I would have answered it. But I answered the last question, that being all I could handle. "I assigned it."

Miles came in. "Where did he put it?"

"He says he's mailed it . . . because he has *assigned* it! You had better find his car and search it—he may just think he actually mailed it. He certainly had it with him at the insurance company."

"Assigned it!" repeated Miles. "Good Lord! To whom?"

"I'll ask him. Dan, to whom did you assign your stock?"

"To the Bank of America." She didn't ask me why or I would have told her about Ricky.

All she did was slump her shoulders and sigh. "There goes the ball game, Chubby. We can forget about the stock. It'll take more than a nail file to get it away from a bank." She straightened up suddenly. "Unless he hasn't really mailed it yet. If he hasn't I'll clean that assignment off the back so pretty you'll think it's been to the laundry. Then he'll assign it again . . . to me."

"To us," corrected Miles.

"That's just a detail. Go find his car."

Miles returned later and announced, "It's not anywhere within six blocks of here. I cruised around all the streets, and the alleys too. He must have used a cab."

"You heard him say he drove his own car."

"Well, it's not out there. Ask him when and where he mailed the stock."

So Belle did and I told them. "Just before I came here. I mailed it at the postbox at the corner of Sepulveda and Ventura Boulevard."

"Do you suppose he's lying?" asked Miles.

"He can't lie, not in the shape he's in. And he's too definite about it to be mixed up. Forget it, Miles. Maybe after he's put away it will turn out that his assignment is no good because he had already sold it to us . . . at least I'll get his signature on some blank sheets and be ready to try it."

She did try to get my signature and I tried to oblige. But in the shape I was in I could not write well enough to satisfy her. Finally she snatched a sheet out of my hand and said viciously, "You make me sick! I can sign your name better than that." Then she leaned over me and said tensely, "I wish I had killed your cat."

They did not bother me again until later in the day. Then Belle came in and said, "Danny boy, I'm going to give you a hypo and then you'll feel a lot better. You'll feel able to get up and move around and act just like you always have acted. You won't be angry at anybody, especially not at Miles and me. We're your best friends. We are, aren't we? Who are your best friends?"

"You are. You and Miles."

"But I'm more than that. I'm your sister. Say it."

"You're my sister."

"Good. Now we're going for a ride and then you are going for a long sleep. You've been sick and when you wake up you'll be well. Understand me?"

"Yes."

"Who am I?"

"You're my best friend. You're my sister."

"Good boy. Push your sleeve back."

I didn't feel the hypo go in, but it stung after she pulled it out. I sat up and shrugged and said, "Gee, Sis, that stung. What was it?"

"Something to make you feel better. You've been sick."

"Yeah, I'm sick. Where's Miles?"

"He'll be here in a moment. Now let's have your other arm. Push back the sleeve."

I said, "What for?" but I pushed back the sleeve and let her shoot me again. I jumped.

She smiled. "That didn't really hurt, did it?"

"Huh? No, it didn't hurt. What's it for?"

"It will make you sleepy on the ride. Then when we get there you'll wake up."

"Okay. I'd like to sleep. I want to take a long sleep." Then I felt puzzled and looked around. "Where's Pete? Pete was going to sleep with me."

"Pete?" Belle said. "Why, dear, don't you remember? You sent Pete to stay with Ricky. She's going to take care of him."

"Oh yes!" I grinned with relief. I had sent Pete to Ricky; I remembered mailing him. That was good. Ricky loved Pete and she would take good care of him while I was asleep.

They drove me out to the Consolidated Sanctuary at Sawtelle, one that many of the smaller insurance companies used—those that didn't have their own. I slept all the way but came awake at once when Belle spoke to me. Miles stayed in his car and she took me in. The girl at the desk looked up and said, "Davis?"

"Yes," agreed Belle. "I'm his sister. Is the representative for Master Insurance here?"

"You'll find him down in Treatment Room Nine—they're ready and waiting. You can give the papers to the man from Master." She looked at me with interest. "He's had his physical examination?"

"Oh yes!" Belle assured her. "Brother is a therapy-delay case, you know. He's under an opiate . . . for the pain."

The receptionist clucked sympathetically. "Well, hurry on in then. Through that door and turn left."

In Room Nine there was a man in street clothes and one in white coveralls and a woman in a nurse's uniform. They helped me get undressed and treated me like an idiot child while Belle explained again that I was under a sedative for the pain. Once he had me stripped and up on the table, the man in white massaged my belly, digging his fingers in deeply. "No trouble with this one," he announced. "He's empty."

"He hasn't had anything to eat or drink since yesterday evening," agreed Belle.

"That's fine. Sometimes they come in here stuffed like a Christmas turkey. Some people have no sense."

"True. Very true."

"Uh-huh. Okay, son, clench your fist tight while I get this needle in."

I did and things began to get really hazy. Suddenly I remembered something and tried to sit up. "Where's Pete? I want to see Pete."

Belle took my head and kissed me. "There, there, Buddy! Pete couldn't come, remember? Pete had to stay with Ricky." I quieted down and she said gently to the others, "Our brother Peter has a sick little girl at home."

I dropped off to sleep.

Presently I felt very cold. But I couldn't move to reach the covers.

V

I was complaining to the bartender about the air conditioning—
it was turned too high and we were all going to catch cold. "No
matter," he assured me. "You won't feel it when you're asleep.
Sleep . . . sleep . . . soup of the evening, beautiful sleep." He
had Belle's face.

"How about a warm drink then?" I wanted to know. "A Tom
and Jerry? Or a hot buttered bum?"

"You're a bum!" the doctor answered. "Sleeping's too good for
him; throw the bum out!"

I tried to hook my feet around the brass rail to stop them. But
this bar had no brass rail, which seemed funny, and I was flat on
my back, which seemed funnier still, unless they had installed
bedside service for people with no feet. I didn't have feet, so how
could I hook them under a brass rail? No hands, either. "Look,
Maw, no hands!" Pete sat on my chest and wailed.

I was back in basic training . . . advanced basic, it must have
been, for I was at Camp Hale at one of those silly exercises where
they throw snow down your neck to make a man of you. I was
having to climb the damnedest biggest mountain in all Colorado
and it was all ice and I had no feet. Nevertheless, I was carrying
the biggest pack anybody ever saw—I remembered that they were
trying to find out if GIs could be used instead of pack mules and

I had been picked because I was expendable. I wouldn't have made it at all if little Ricky hadn't got behind me and pushed.

The top sergeant turned and he had a face just like Belle's and he was livid with rage. "Come on, you! I can't afford to wait for you. I don't care whether you make it or not . . . but you can't sleep until you get there."

My no-feet wouldn't take me any farther and I fell down in the snow and it was icy warm and I did fall asleep while little Ricky wailed and begged me not to. But I had to sleep.

I woke up in bed with Belle. She was shaking me and saying, "Wake up, Dan! I can't wait thirty years for you; a girl has to think of her future." I tried to get up and hand her the bags of gold I had under the bed, but she was gone . . . and anyhow a *Hired Girl* with her face had picked all the gold up and put it in its tray on top and scurried out of the room. I tried to run after it but I had no feet, no body at all, I discovered. "I ain't got no body, and nobody cares for me. . . ." The world consisted of top sergeants and work . . . so what difference did it make where you worked or how? I let them put the harness back on me and I went back to climbing that icy mountain. It was all white and beautifully rounded and if I could just climb to the rosy tip they would let me sleep, which was what I needed. But I never made it . . . no hands, no feet, no nothing.

There was a forest fire on the mountain. The snow did not melt, but I could feel the heat in waves beating against me while I kept on struggling. The top sergeant was leaning over me and saying, "Wake up . . . wake up . . . wake up."

He no more than got me awake before he wanted me to sleep again. I'm vague about what happened then for a while. Part of the time I was on a table which vibrated under me and there were lights and snaky-looking equipment and lots of people. But when I was fully awake I was in a hospital bed and I felt all right except for that listless half-floating feeling you have after a Turkish bath. I had hands and feet again. But nobody would talk to me and every time I tried to ask a question a nurse would pop something into my mouth. I was massaged quite a lot.

Then one morning I felt fine and got out of bed as soon as I woke up. I felt a little dizzy but that was all. I knew who I was,

I knew how I had got there, and I knew that all that other stuff had been dreams.

I knew who had put me there. If Belle had given me orders while I was drugged to forget her shenanigans, either the orders had not taken or thirty years of cold sleep had washed out the hypnotic effect. I was blurry about some details but I knew how they had shanghaied me.

I wasn't especially angry about it. True, it had happened just "yesterday," since yesterday is the day just one sleep behind you—but the sleep had been thirty years long. The feeling cannot be precisely defined, since it is entirely subjective, but, while my memory was sharp for the events of "yesterday," nevertheless my feelings about those events were to things far away. You have seen double images in television of a pitcher making his windup while his picture sits as a ghost on top of a long shot of the whole baseball diamond? Something like that . . . my conscious recollection was a close-up; my emotional reaction was to something long ago and far away.

I fully intended to look up Belle and Miles and chop them into cat meat, but there was no hurry. Next year would do—right now I was eager to have a look at the year 2000.

But speaking of cat meat, where was Pete? He ought to be around somewhere . . . unless the poor little beggar hadn't lived through the Sleep.

Then—and not until then—did I remember that my careful plans to bring Pete along had been wrecked.

I took Belle and Miles out of the "Hold" basket and moved them over to "Urgent." Try to kill my cat, would they?

They had done worse than kill Pete; they had turned him out to go wild . . . to wear out his days wandering back alleys in search of scraps, while his ribs grew thin and his sweet pixie nature warped into distrust of all two-legged beasts.

They had let him die—for he was surely dead by now—let him die thinking that *I* had deserted him.

For this they would pay . . . if they were still alive. Oh, how I hoped they were still alive—*unspeakable!*

I found that I was standing by the foot of my bed, grasping the rail to steady myself and dressed only in pajamas. I looked around for some way to call someone. Hospital rooms had not changed much. There was no window and I could not see where the light came from; the bed was high and narrow, as hospital beds had always been in my recollection, but it showed signs of having been engineered into something more than a place to sleep —among other things, it seemed to have some sort of plumbing under it which I suspected was a mechanized bedpan, and the side table was part of the bed structure itself. But, while I ordinarily would have been intensely interested in such gadgetry, right now I simply wanted to find the pear-shaped switch which summons the nurse—I wanted my clothes.

It was missing, but I found what it had been transformed into: a pressure switch on the side of the table that was not quite a table. My hand struck it in trying to find it, and a transparency opposite where my head would have been had I been in bed shone out with: SERVICE CALL. Almost immediately it blinked out and was replaced with: ONE MOMENT, PLEASE.

Very quickly the door silently rolled aside and a nurse came in. Nurses had not changed much. This one was reasonably cute, had the familiar firm manners of a drill sergeant, wore a perky little white hat perched on short orchid-colored hair, and was dressed in a white uniform. It was strangely cut and covered her here and uncovered her there in a fashion different from 1970— but women's clothes, even work uniforms, were always doing that. She would still have been a nurse in any year, just by her unmistakable manner.

"You get back in that bed!"

"Where are my clothes?"

"Get back in that bed. Now!"

I answered reasonably, "Look, nurse, I'm a free citizen, over twenty-one, and not a criminal. I don't have to get back into that bed and I'm not going to. Now are you going to show me where my clothes are or shall I go out the way I am and start looking?"

She looked at me, then turned suddenly and went out; the door ducked out of her way.

But it would not duck out of my way. I was still trying to study out the gimmick, being fairly sure that if one engineer could dream it up, another could figure it out, when it opened again and a man came in.

"Good morning," he said. "I'm Dr. Albrecht."

His clothes looked like a cross between a Harlem Sunday and a picnic to me, but his brisk manner and his tired eyes were convincingly professional; I believed him. "Good morning, Doctor. I'd like to have my clothes."

He stepped just far enough inside to let the door slide into place behind him, then reached inside his clothes and pulled out a pack of cigarettes. He got one out, waved it briskly in the air, placed it in his mouth and puffed on it; it was lighted. He offered me the pack. "Have one?"

"Uh, no, thanks."

"Go ahead. It won't hurt you."

I shook my head. I had always worked with a cigarette smoldering beside me; the progress of a job could be judged by the overflowing ash trays and the burns on the drafting board. Now I felt a little faint at the sight of smoke and wondered if I had dropped the nicotine habit somewhere in the slept-away years. "Thanks just the same."

"Okay. Mr. Davis, I've been here six years. I'm a specialist in hypnology, resuscitation, and like subjects. Here and elsewhere I've helped eight thousand and seventy-three patients make the comeback from hypothermia to normal life—you're number eight thousand and seventy-four. I've seen them do all sorts of odd things when they came out—odd to laymen; not to me. Some of them want to go right back to sleep again and scream at me when I try to keep them awake. Some of them *do* go back to sleep and we have to ship them off to another sort of institution. Some of them start weeping endlessly when they realize that it is a one-way ticket and it's too late to go home to whatever year they started from. And some of them, like you, demand their clothes and want to run out into the street."

"Well? Why not? Am I a prisoner?"

"No. You can have your clothes. I imagine you'll find them out of style, but that is your problem. However, while I send for them, would you mind telling me what it is that is so terribly urgent that you must attend to it right this minute . . . after it has waited thirty years? That's how long you've been at subtemperature—thirty years. Is it really urgent? Or would later today do as well? Or even tomorrow?"

I started to blurt out that it damn well was urgent, then stopped and looked sheepish. "Maybe not that urgent."

"Then as a favor to me, will you get back into bed, let me check you over, have your breakfast, and perhaps talk with me before you go galloping off in all directions? I might even be able to tell you which way to gallop."

"Uh, okay, Doctor. Sorry to have caused trouble." I climbed into bed. It felt good—I was suddenly tired and shaky.

"No trouble. You should see some that we get. We have to pull them down off the ceiling." He straightened the covers around my shoulders, then leaned over the table built into the bed. "Dr. Albrecht in Seventeen. Send a room orderly with breakfast, uh . . . menu four-minus."

He turned to me and said, "Roll over and pull up your jacket; I want to get at your ribs. While I'm checking you, you can ask questions. If you want to."

I tried to think while he prodded my ribs. I suppose it was a stethoscope he used although it looked like a miniaturized hearing aid. But they had not improved one thing about it; the pickup he pushed against me was as cold and hard as ever.

What do you ask after thirty years? Have they reached the stars yet? Who's cooking up "The War to End War" this time? Do babies come out of test tubes? "Doc, do they still have popcorn machines in the lobbies of movie theaters?"

"They did the last time I looked. I don't get much time for such things. By the way, the word is 'grabbie' now, not 'movie.'"

"So? Why?"

"Try one. You'll find out. But be sure to fasten your seat belt; they null the whole theater on some shots. See here, Mr. Davis, we're faced with this same problem every day and we've got it down to a routine. We've got adjustment vocabularies for each entrance year, and historical and cultural summaries. It's quite necessary, for malorientation can be extreme no matter how much we lackweight the shock."

"Uh, I suppose so."

"Decidedly. Especially in an extreme lapse like yours. Thirty years."

"Is thirty years the maximum?"

"Yes and no. Thirty-five years is the very longest we've had experience with, since the first commercial client was placed in subtemperature in December 1965. You are the longest Sleeper I have revived. But we have clients in here now with contract times up to a century and a half. They should never have accepted you for as long as thirty years; they didn't know enough then. They were taking a great chance with your life. You were lucky."

"Really?"

"Really. Turn over." He went on examining me and added, "But with what we've learned now I'd be willing to prepare a man for a thousand-year jump if there were any way to finance it . . . hold him at the temperature you were at for a year just to check, then crash him to minus two hundred in a millisecond. He'd live. I think. Let's try your reflexes."

That "crash" business didn't sound good to me. Dr. Albrecht went on: "Sit up and cross your knees. You won't find the language problem difficult. Of course I've been careful to talk in 1970 vocabulary—I rather pride myself on being able to talk selectively in the entrance speech of any of my patients; I've made a hypnostudy of it. But you'll be speaking contemporary idiom perfectly in a week; it's really just added vocabulary."

I thought of telling him that at least four times he had used words not used in 1970, or at least not that way, but I decided it wouldn't be polite. "That's all for now," he said presently. "By the way, Mrs. Schultz has been trying to reach you."

"Huh?"

"Don't you know her? She insisted that she was an old friend of yours."

" 'Schultz,' " I repeated. "I suppose I've known several 'Mrs. Schultzes' at one time and another, but the only one I can place was my fourth-grade teacher. But she'd be dead by now."

"Maybe she took the Sleep. Well, you can accept the message when you feel like it. I'm going to sign a release on you. But if you're smart, you'll stay here for a few days and soak up reorientation. I'll look in on you later. So 'twenty-three, skiddoo!' as they used to say in your day. Here comes the orderly with your breakfast."

I decided that he was a better doctor than a linguist. But I stopped thinking about it when I saw the orderly. It rolled in, carefully avoiding Dr. Albrecht, who walked straight out, paying no attention to it and making no effort himself to avoid it.

It came over, adjusted the built-in bed table, swung it over me, opened it out, and arranged my breakfast on it. "Shall I pour your coffee?"

"Yes, please." I did not really want it poured, as I would rather have it stay hot until I've finished everything else. But I wanted to see it poured.

For I was in a delighted daze . . . it was *Flexible Frank!*

Not the jackleg, bread-boarded, jury-rigged first model Miles and Belle had stolen from me, of course not. This one resembled the first *Frank* the way a turbospeedster resembles the first horseless carriages. But a man knows his own work. I had set the basic pattern and this was the necessary evolution . . . *Frank's* great-grandson, improved, slicked up, made more efficient—but the same bloodline.

"Will that be all?"

"Wait a minute."

Apparently I had said the wrong thing, for the automaton reached inside itself and pulled out a stiff plastic sheet and handed it to me. The sheet remained fastened to him by a slim steel chain. I looked at it and found printed on it:

VOICE CODE—Eager Beaver Model XVII-a

IMPORTANT NOTICE!! This service automaton DOES NOT understand human speech. It has no understanding at all, being merely a machine. But for your convenience it has been designed to respond to a list of spoken orders. It will ignore anything else said in its presence, or (if any phrase triggers it incompletely or such that a circuit dilemma is created) it will offer this instruction sheet. Please read it carefully.

> *Thank you,*
> *Aladdin Autoengineering Corporation*
> *Manufacturers of EAGER BEA-*
> *VER, WILLIWAW, DRAFTING*
> *DAN, BUILDER BILL, GREEN*
> *THUMB, and NANNY. Custom*

"At Your Service!"

The motto appeared on their trade-mark showing Aladdin rubbing his lamp and a genie appearing.

Below this was a long list of simple orders—STOP, GO, YES, NO, SLOWER, FASTER, COME HERE, FETCH A NURSE, etc. Then there was a shorter list of tasks common in hospitals, such as back rubs, and including some that I had never heard of. The list closed abruptly with the statement: "Routines 87 through 242 may be ordered only by hospital staff members and the order phrases are therefore not listed here."

I had not voice-coded the first *Flexible Frank;* you had to punch buttons on his control board. It was not because I had not thought of it, but because the analyzer and telephone exchange for the purpose would have weighed and bulked and cost more than all the rest of *Frank, Sr.,* net. I decided that I would have to learn some new wrinkles in miniaturization and simplification before I would be ready to practice engineering here. But I was anxious to get started on it, as I could see from *Eager Beaver* that it was going to be more fun than ever—lots of new possibilities. Engineering is the art of the practical and depends more on the total state of the art than it does on the individual engineer. When railroading time comes you can railroad—but not before. Look at poor Professor Langley, breaking his heart on a flying machine that should have flown—he had put the necessary genius in it—but he was just a few years too early to enjoy the benefit of collateral art he needed and did not have. Or take the great Leonardo da Vinci, so far out of his time that his most brilliant concepts were utterly unbuildable.

I was going to have fun here—I mean "now."

I handed back the instruction card, then got out of bed and looked for the data plate. I had halfway expected to see "Hired Girl, Inc." at the bottom of the notice and I wondered if "Aladdin" was a daughter corporation of the Mannix group. The data plate did not tell me much other than model, serial number, factory, and such, but it did list the patents, about forty of them—and the earliest, I was *very* interested to see, was in 1970 . . . almost certainly based on my original model and drawings.

I found a pencil and memo pad on the table and jotted down the number of that first patent, but my interest was purely intellectual. Even if it had been stolen from me (I was sure it had been), it had expired in 1987—unless they had changed the patent laws—and only those granted later than 1983 would still be valid. But I wanted to know.

A light glowed on the automaton and he announced: "I am being called. May I leave?"

"Huh? Sure. Run along." It started to reach for the phrase list; I hastily said, "Go!"

"Thank you. Good-by." It detoured around me.

"Thank *you*."

"You are welcome."

Whoever had dictated the gadget's sound responses had a very pleasant baritone voice.

I got back into bed and ate the breakfast I had let get cold—only it turned out not to be cold. Breakfast four-minus was about enough for a medium-sized bird, but I found that it was enough, even though I had been very hungry. I suppose my stomach had shrunk. It wasn't until I had finished that I remembered that this was the first food I had eaten in a generation. I noticed it then because they had included a menu—what I had taken for bacon was listed as "grilled yeast strips, country style."

But in spite of a thirty-year fast, my mind was not on food; they had sent a newspaper in with breakfast: the Great Los Angeles *Times,* for Wednesday, 13 December, 2000.

Newspapers had not changed much, not in format. This one was tabloid size, the paper was glazed instead of rough pulp and the illustrations were either full color, or black-and-white stereo—I couldn't puzzle out the gimmick on that last. There had been stereo pictures you could look at without a viewer since I was a small child; as a kid I had been fascinated by ones used to advertise frozen foods in the '50s. But those had required fairly thick transparent plastic for a grid of tiny prisms; these were simply on thin paper. Yet they had depth.

I gave it up and looked at the rest of the paper. *Eager Beaver* had arranged it on a reading rack and for a while it seemed as if the front page was all I was going to read, for I could not find out how to open the durned thing. The sheets seemed to have frozen solid.

Finally I accidentally touched the lower right-hand corner of the first sheet; it curled up and out of the way . . . some surface-charge phenomenon, triggered at that point. The other pages got neatly out of the way in succession whenever I touched that spot.

At least half of the paper was so familiar as to make me home-sick—"Your Horoscope Today, Mayor Dedicates New Reservoir, Security Restrictions Undermining Freedom of Press Says N.Y. Solon, Giants Take Double-Header, Unseasonable Warmth Perils Winter Sports, Pakistan Warns India"—et cetera, ad tedium. This is where I came in.

Some of the other items were new but explained themselves: LUNA SHUTTLE STILL SUSPENDED FOR GEMINIDS —*Twenty-Four-Hour Station Suffers Two Punctures, No Casualties;* FOUR WHITES LYNCHED IN CAPETOWN—*UN Action Demanded;* HOST-MOTHERS ORGANIZE FOR HIGHER FEES—*Demand "Amateurs" Be Outlawed;* MISSISSIPPI PLANTER INDICTED UNDER ANTI-ZOMBIE LAW—*His Defense: "Them Boys Hain't Drugged, They're Just Stupid!"*

I was fairly sure that I knew what that last one meant . . . from experience.

But some of the news items missed me completely. The "wogglies" were still spreading and three more French towns had been evacuated; the King was considering ordering the area dusted. King? Oh well, French politics might turn up anything, but what was this "Poudre Sanitaire" they were considering using on the "wogglies"?—whatever they were. Radioactive, maybe? I hoped they picked a dead calm day . . . preferably the thirtieth of February. I had had a radiation overdose myself once, through a mistake by a damn-fool WAC technician at Sandia. I had not reached the point-of-no-return vomiting stage, but I don't recommend a diet of curies.

The Laguna Beach division of the Los Angeles police had been equipped with Leycoils and the division chief warned all Teddies to get out of town. "My men have orders to nark first and subspeck afterward. This has got to stop!"

I made a mental note to keep clear of Laguna Beach until I found out what the score was. I wasn't sure I wanted to be sub-specked, or subspected, even afterward.

Those are just samples. There were any number of news stories that started out trippingly, then foundered in what was, to me, double talk.

I started to breeze on past the vital statistics when my eye caught some new subheads. There were the old familiar ones of births, deaths, marriages, and divorces, but now there were "commitments" and "withdrawals" as well, listed by sanctuaries. I looked up "Sawtelle Cons. Sanc." and found my own name. It gave me a warm feeling of "belonging."

But the most intensely interesting things in the paper were the ads. One of the personals stuck in my mind: "Attractive still-young widow with yen to travel wishes to meet mature man similarly inclined. Object: two-year marriage contract." But it was the display advertising that got me.

Hired Girl and her sisters and her cousins and her aunts were all over the place—and they were still using the trade-mark, a husky girl with a broom, that I had designed originally for our letterhead. I felt a twinge of regret that I had been in such a jumping hurry to get rid of my stock in Hired Girl, Inc.; it looked as if it was worth more than all the rest of my portfolio. No, that was wrong; if I had kept it with me at the time, that pair of thieves would have lifted it and faked an assignment to themselves. As it was, Ricky had gotten it—and if it had made Ricky rich, well, it couldn't happen to a nicer person.

I made a note to track down Ricky first thing, top priority. She was all that was left to me of the world I had known and she loomed very large in my mind. Dear little Ricky! If she had been ten years older I would never have looked at Belle . . . and wouldn't have got my fingers burned.

Let's see, how old would she be now? Forty—no, forty-one. It was hard to think of Ricky as forty-one. Still, that wouldn't be old in a woman these days—or even those days. From forty feet you frequently couldn't tell forty-one from eighteen.

If she was rich I'd let her buy me a drink and we would drink to Pete's dear departed funny little soul.

And if something had slipped and she was poor in spite of the stock I had assigned her, then—by damn, I'd marry her! Yes, I would. It didn't matter that she was ten years or so older than I was; in view of my established record for flubbing the dub I needed somebody older to look out for me and tell me no—and Ricky was just the girl who could do it. She had run Miles and Miles's house with serious little-girl efficiency when she was less than ten; at forty she would be just the same, only mellowed.

I felt really warm and no longer lost in a strange land for the first time since I had wakened. Ricky was the answer to everything.

Then deep inside me I heard a voice: "Look, stupid, you can't marry Ricky, because a girl as sweet as she was going to be would now have been married for at least twenty years. She'll have four kids . . . maybe a son bigger than you are . . . and certainly a husband who won't be amused by you in the role of good old Uncle Danny."

I listened and my jaw sagged. Then I said feebly, "All right, all right—so I've missed the boat again. But I'm still going to look her up. They can't do more than shoot me. And, after all, she's the only other person who really understood Pete."

I turned another page, suddenly very glum at the thought of having lost both Ricky and Pete. After a while I fell asleep over the paper and slept until *Eager Beaver* or his twin fetched lunch.

While I was asleep I dreamed that Ricky was holding me on her lap and saying, "It's all right, Danny. I found Pete and now we're both here to stay. Isn't that so, Pete?"

"*Yeeeow!*"

The added vocabularies were a cinch; I spent much more time on the historical summaries. Quite a lot can happen in thirty years, but why put it down when everybody else knows it better than I do? I wasn't surprised that the Great Asia Republic was crowding us out of the South American trade; that had been in the cards since the Formosan treaty. Nor was I surprised to find India more Balkanized than ever. The notion of England being a province of Canada stopped me for a moment. Which was the tail and which was the dog? I skipped over the panic of '87; gold was a wonderful engineering material for some uses; I could not regard it as a tragedy to find that it was now cheap and no longer a basis for money, no matter how many people lost their shirts in the change-over.

I stopped reading and thought about the things you could do with cheap gold, with its high density, good conductivity, extreme ductility . . . and stopped when I realized I would have to read the technical literature first. Shucks, in atomics alone it would be invaluable. The way the stuff could be worked, far better than any other metal, if you could use it in miniaturizing—again I stopped, morally certain that *Eager Beaver* had had his "head" crammed full of gold. I would just have to get busy and find out what the boys had been doing in the "small back rooms" while I had been away.

The Sawtelle Sanctuary wasn't equipped to let me read up on engineering, so I told Doc Albrecht I was ready to check out. He shrugged, told me I was an idiot, and agreed. But I did stay one more night; I found that I was fagged just from lying back and watching words chase past in a book scanner.

They brought me modern clothes right after breakfast the next morning . . . and I had to have help in dressing. They were not so odd in themselves (although I had never worn cerise trousers with bell bottoms before) but I could not manage the fastenings without coaching. I suppose my grandfather might have had the same trouble with zippers if he had not been led into them gradually. It was the Sticktite closure seams, of course—I thought I was going to have to hire a little boy to help me go to the bathroom before I got it through my head that the pressure-sensitive adhesion was axially polarized.

Then I almost lost my pants when I tried to ease the waistband. No one laughed at me.

Dr. Albrecht asked, "What are you going to do?"

"Me? First I'm going to get a map of the city. Then I'm going to find a place to sleep. Then I'm going to do nothing but professional reading for quite a while . . . maybe a year. Doc, I'm an obsolete engineer. I don't aim to stay that way."

"Mmmm. Well, good luck. Don't hesitate to call if I can help."

I stuck out my hand. "Thanks, Doc. You've been swell. Uh,

maybe I shouldn't mention this until I talk to the accounting office of my insurance company and see just how well off I am—but I don't intend to let it go with words. Thanks for the sort of thing you've done for me should be more substantial. Understand me?"

He shook his head. "I appreciate the thought. But my fees are covered by my contract with the sanctuary."

"But——"

"No. I can't take it, so please let's not discuss it." He shook hands and said, "Good-by. If you'll stay on this slide it will take you to the main offices." He hesitated. "If you find things a bit tiring at first, you're entitled to four more days recuperation and reorientation here without additional charge under the custodial contract. It's paid for. Might as well use it. You can come and go as you like."

I grinned. "Thanks, Doc. But you can bet that I won't be back —other than to say hello someday."

I stepped off at the main office and told the receptionist there who I was. It handed me an envelope, which I saw was another phone message from Mrs. Schultz. I still had not called her, because I did not know who she was, and the sanctuary did not permit visits nor phone calls to a revivified client until he wanted to accept them. I simply glanced at it and tucked it in my blouse, while thinking that I might have made a mistake in making *Flexible Frank* too flexible. Receptionists used to be pretty girls, not machines.

The receptionist said, "Step this way, please. Our treasurer would like to see you."

Well, I wanted to see him, too, so I stepped that way. I was wondering how much money I had made and was congratulating myself on having plunged in common stocks rather than playing it "safe." No doubt my stocks had dropped in the Panic of '87, but they ought to be back up now—in fact I knew that at least two of them were worth a lot of dough now; I had been reading the financial section of the *Times*. I still had the paper with me, figuring I might want to look up some others.

The treasurer was a human being, even though he looked like a treasurer. He gave me a quick handshake. "How do you do, Mr. Davis. I'm Mr. Doughty. Sit down, please."

I said, "Howdy, Mr. Doughty. I probably don't need to take

that much of your time. Just tell me this: does my insurance company handle its settlements through your office? Or should I go to their home offices?"

"Do please sit down. I have several things to explain to you."

So I sat. His office assistant (good old *Frank* again) fetched a file folder for him and he said, "These are your original contracts. Would you like to see them?"

I wanted very much to see them, as I had kept my fingers crossed ever since I was fully awake, wondering if Belle had figured out some way to bite the end off that certified check. A certified check is much harder to play hanky-panky with than is a personal check, but Belle was a clever gal.

I was much relieved to see that she had left my commitments unchanged, except of course that the side contract for Pete was missing and also the one concerning my Hired Girl stock. I supposed that she had just burned those, to keep from raising questions. I examined with care the dozen or more places where she had changed "Mutual Assurance Company" to "Master Insurance Company of California."

The gal was a real artist, no question. I suppose a scientific criminologist armed with microscope and comparison stereo and chemical tests and so forth could have proved that each of those documents had been altered, but I could not. I wondered how she had coped with the closed endorsement on the back of the certified check, since certified checks are always on paper guaranteed non-erasable. Well, she probably had not used an eraser—what one person can dream up another person can outsmart . . . and Belle was *very* smart.

Mr. Doughty cleared his throat. I looked up. "Do we settle my account here?"

"Yes."

"Then I can put it in two words. How much?"

"Mmm . . . Mr. Davis, before we go into that question, I would like to invite your attention to one additional document . . . and to one circumstance. This is the contract between this sanctuary and Master Insurance Company of California for your hypothermia, custody, and revivification. You will note that the entire fee is paid in advance. This is both for our protection and for yours, since it guarantees your safe-being while you are helpless.

The funds—all such funds—are placed in escrow with the superior-court division handling chancery matters and are paid quarterly to us as earned."

"Okay. Sounds like a good arrangement."

"It is. It protects the helpless. Now you must understand clearly that this sanctuary is a separate corporation from your insurance company; the custodial contract with us was a contract entirely separate from the one for the management of your estate."

"Mr. Doughty, what are you getting at?"

"Do you have any assets other than those you entrusted to Master Insurance Company?"

I thought it over. I had owned a car once . . . but God alone knew what had become of it. I had closed out my checking account in Mojave early in the binge, and on that busy day when I ended up at Miles's place—and in the soup—I had started with maybe thirty or forty dollars in cash. Books, clothes, slide rule—I had never been a pack rat—and that minor junk was gone anyhow. "Not even a bus transfer, Mr. Doughty."

"Then—I am very sorry to have to tell you this—you have no assets of any sort."

I held still while my head circled the field and came in for a crash landing. "What do you mean? Why, some of the stocks I invested in are in fine shape. I *know* they are. It says so right here." I held up my breakfast copy of the *Times.*

He shook his head. "I'm sorry, Mr. Davis, but you don't own any stocks. Master Insurance went broke."

I was glad he had made me sit down; I felt weak. "How did this happen? The Panic?"

"No, no. It was part of the collapse of the Mannix Group . . . but of course you don't know about that. It happened after the Panic, and I suppose you could say that it started from the Panic. But Master Insurance would not have gone under if it had not been systematically looted . . . gutted—'milked' is the vulgar word. If it had been an ordinary receivership, something at least would have been salvaged. But it was not. By the time it was discovered there was nothing left of the company but a hollow shell . . . and the men who had done it were beyond extradition. Uh, if it is any consolation to you, it could not happen under our present laws."

No, it was no consolation, and besides, I didn't believe it. My old man claimed that the more complicated the law the more opportunity for scoundrels.

But he also used to say that a wise man should be prepared to abandon his baggage at any time. I wondered how often I was going to have to do it to qualify as "wise." "Uh, Mr. Doughty, just out of curiosity, how did Mutual Assurance make out?"

"Mutual Assurance Company? A fine firm. Oh, they took their licking during the Panic along with everybody else. But they weathered it. You have a policy with them, perhaps?"

"No." I did not offer explanation; there was no use. I couldn't look to Mutual; I had never executed my contract with them. I couldn't sue Master Insurance; there is no point in suing a bankrupt corpse.

I could sue Belle and Miles if they were still around—but why be silly? No proof, none.

Besides, I did not want to sue Belle. It would be better to tattoo her all over with "Null and Void" . . . using a dull needle. Then I'd take up the matter of what she had done to Pete. I hadn't figured out a punishment to suit the crime for that one yet.

I suddenly remembered that it was the Mannix group that Miles and Belle had been about to sell Hired Girl, Inc., to when they had booted me out. "Mr. Doughty? Are you sure that the Mannix people haven't any assets? Don't they own Hired Girl?"

" 'Hired Girl?' Do you mean the domestic autoappliance firm?"

"Yes, of course."

"It hardly seems possible. In fact, it is not possible, since the Mannix empire, as such, no longer exists. Of course I can't say that there never was any connection between Hired Girl Corporation and the Mannix people. But I don't believe it could have been much, if any, or I think I would have heard of it."

I dropped the matter. If Miles and Belle had been caught in the collapse of Mannix, that suited me fine. But, on the other hand, if Mannix had owned and milked Hired Girl, Inc., it would have hit Ricky as hard as it hit them. I didn't want Ricky hurt, no matter what the side issues were.

I stood up. "Well, thanks for breaking it gently, Mr. Doughty. I'll be on my way."

"Don't go yet. Mr. Davis . . . we of this institution feel a responsibility toward our people beyond the mere letter of the contract. You understand that yours is by no means the first case of this sort. Now our board of directors has placed a small discretionary fund at my disposal to ease such hardships. It——"

"No charity, Mr. Doughty. Thanks anyhow."

"Not charity, Mr. Davis. A loan. A character loan, you might call it. Believe me, our losses have been negligible on such loans . . . and we don't want you to walk out of here with your pockets empty."

I thought that one over twice. I didn't even have the price of a haircut. On the other hand, borrowing money is like trying to swim with a brick in each hand . . . and a small loan is tougher to pay back than a million. "Mr. Doughty," I said slowly, "Dr. Albrecht said that I was entitled to four more days of beans and bed here."

"I believe that is right—I'd have to consult your card. Not that we throw people out even when their contract time is up if they are not ready."

"I didn't suppose that you did. But what are the rates on that room I had, as hospital room and board?"

"Eh? But our rooms are not for rent in that way. We aren't a hospital; we simply maintain a recovery infirmary for our clients."

"Yes, surely. But you must figure it, at least for cost accounting purposes."

"Mmm . . . yes and no. The figures aren't allocated on that basis. The subheads are depreciation, overhead, operation, reserves, diet kitchen, personnel, and so forth. I suppose I could make an estimate."

"Uh, don't bother. What would equivalent room and board in a hospital come to?"

"That's a little out of my line. Still . . . well, you could call it about one hundred dollars per day, I suppose."

"I had four days coming. Will you lend me four hundred dollars?"

He did not answer but spoke in a number code to his mechanical assistant. Then eight fifty-dollar bills were being counted into my hand. "Thanks," I said sincerely as I tucked it away.

"I'll do my damnedest to see that this does not stay on the books too long. Six per cent? Or is money tight?"

He shook his head. "It's not a loan. Since you put it as you did, I canceled it against your unused time."

"Huh? Now, see here, Mr. Doughty, I didn't intend to twist your arm. Of course, I'm going to——"

"Please. I told my assistant to enter the charge when I directed it to pay you. Do you want to give our auditors headaches all for a fiddling four hundred dollars? I was prepared to loan you much more than that."

"Well— I can't argue it now. Say, Mr. Doughty, how much money is this? How are price levels now?"

"Mmm . . . that is a complex question."

"Just give me an idea? What does it cost to eat?"

"Food is quite reasonable. For ten dollars you can get a very satisfactory dinner . . . if you are careful to select moderate-priced restaurants."

I thanked him and left with a really warm feeling. Mr. Doughty reminded me of a paymaster I used to have in the Army. Paymasters come in only two sizes: one sort shows you where the book says that you can't have what you've got coming to you; the second sort digs through the book until he finds a paragraph that lets you have what you need even if you don't rate it.

Doughty was the second sort.

The sanctuary faced on the Wilshire Ways. There were benches in front of it and bushes and flowers. I sat down on a bench to take stock and to decide whether to go east or west. I had kept a stiff lip with Mr. Doughty but, honestly, I was badly shaken, even though I had the price of a week's meals in my jeans.

But the sun was warm and the drone of the Ways was pleasant and I was young (biologically at least) and I had two hands and my brain. Whistling "Hallelujah, I'm a bum," I opened the *Times* to the "Help Wanted" columns.

I resisted the impulse to look through "Professional—Engineers" and turned at once to "Unskilled."

That classification was darned short. I almost couldn't find it.

VI

I got a job the second day, Friday, the fifteenth of December. I also had a mild run-in with the law and had repeated tangles with new ways of doing things, saying things, feeling about things. I discovered that "reorientation" by reading about it is like reading about sex—not the same thing.

I suppose I would have had less trouble if I had been set down in Omsk, or Santiago, or Djakarta. In going to a strange city in a strange land you *know* that the customs are going to be different, but in Great Los Angeles I subconsciously expected things to be unchanged even though I could see that they were changed. Of course thirty years is nothing; anybody takes that much change and more in a lifetime. But it makes a difference to take it in one bite.

Take one word I used all in innocence. A lady present was offended and only the fact that I was a Sleeper—which I hastily explained—kept her husband from giving me a mouthful of knuckles. I won't use the word here—oh yes, I will; why shouldn't I? I'm using it to explain something. Don't take my word for it that the word was in good usage when I was a kid; look it up in an old dictionary. Nobody scrawled it in chalk on sidewalks when I was a kid.

The word was "kink."

There were other words which I still do not use properly without stopping to think. Not taboo words necessarily, just ones with changed meanings. "Host" for example—"host" used to mean the man who took your coat and put it in the bedroom; it had nothing to do with the birth rate.

But I got along. The job I found was crushing new ground limousines so that they could be shipped back to Pittsburgh as scrap. Cadillacs, Chryslers, Eisenhowers, Lincolns—all sorts of great, big, new powerful turbobuggies without a kilometer on their clocks. Drive 'em between the jaws, then *crunch! smash! crash!*—scrap iron for blast furnaces.

It hurt me at first, since I was riding the Ways to work and didn't own so much as a gravJumper. I expressed my opinion of it and almost lost my job . . . until the shift boss remembered that I was a Sleeper and really didn't understand.

"It's a simple matter of economics, son. These are surplus cars the government has accepted as security against price-support loans. They're two years old now and they can never be sold . . . so the government junks them and sells them back to the steel industry. You can't run a blast furnace just on ore; you have to have scrap iron as well. You ought to know that even if you are a Sleeper. Matter of fact, with high-grade ore so scarce, there's more and more demand for scrap. The steel industry needs these cars."

"But why build them in the first place if they can't be sold? It seems wasteful."

"It just *seems* wasteful. You want to throw people out of work? You want to run down the standard of living?"

"Well, why not ship them abroad? It seems to me they could get more for them on the open market abroad than they are worth as scrap."

"What!—and ruin the export market? Besides, if we started dumping cars abroad we'd get everybody sore at us—Japan, France, Germany, Great Asia, everybody. What are you aiming to do? Start a war?" He sighed and went on in a fatherly tone. "You go down to the public library and draw out some books. You don't have any right to opinions on these things until you know something about them."

So I shut up. I didn't tell him that I was spending all my off time at the public library or at U.C.L.A.'s library; I had avoided admitting that I was, or used to be, an engineer—to claim that I was now an engineer would be too much like walking up to du Pont's and saying, "Sirrah, I am an alchymiste. Hast need of art such as mine?"

I raised the subject just once more because I noticed that very few of the price-support cars were really ready to run. The workmanship was sloppy and they often lacked essentials like instrument dials or air conditioners. But when one day I noticed from the way the teeth of the crusher came down on one that it lacked even a power plant, I spoke up about it.

The shift boss just stared at me. "Great jumping Jupiter, son, surely you don't expect them to put their best workmanship into cars that are just surplus? These cars had price-support loans against them before they ever came off the assembly line."

So that time I shut up and stayed shut. I had better stick to engineering; economics is too esoteric for me.

But I had plenty of time to think. The job I had was not really a "job" at all in my book; all the work was done by *Flexible Frank* in his various disguises. *Frank* and his brothers ran the crusher, moved the cars into place, hauled away the scrap, kept count, and weighed the loads; my job was to stand on a little platform (I wasn't allowed to sit) and hang onto a switch that could stop the whole operation if something went wrong. Nothing ever did, but I soon found that I was expected to spot at least one failure in automation each shift, stop the job, and send for a trouble crew.

Well, it paid twenty-one dollars a day and it kept me eating. First things first.

After social security, guild dues, income tax, defense tax, medical plan, and the welfare mutual fund I took home about sixteen of it. Mr. Doughty was wrong about a dinner costing ten dollars; you could get a very decent plate dinner for three if you did not insist on real meat, and I would defy anyone to tell whether a hamburger steak started life in a tank or out on the open range. With the stories going around about bootleg meat that might give you radiation poisoning I was perfectly happy with surrogates.

Where to live had been somewhat of a problem. Since Los Angeles had not been treated to the one-second slum-clearance plan in the Six Weeks War, an amazing number of refugees had gone there (I suppose I was one of them, although I hadn't thought of myself as such at the time) and apparently none of them had ever gone home, even those that had homes left to go back to. The city—if you can call Great Los Angeles a city; it is more of a condition—had been choked when I went to sleep; now it was as jammed as a lady's purse. It may have been a mistake to get rid of the smog; back in the '60s a few people used to leave each year because of sinusitis.

Now apparently nobody left, ever.

The day I checked out of the sanctuary I had had several things on my mind, principally (1) find a job, (2) find a place to sleep, (3) catch up in engineering, (4) find Ricky, (5) get back into engineering—on my own if humanly possible, (6) find Belle and Miles and settle their hash—without going to jail for it, and (7) a slug of things, like looking up the original patent on *Eager Beaver* and checking my strong hunch that it was really *Flexible Frank* (not that it mattered now, just curiosity), and looking up the corporate history of Hired Girl, Inc., etc., etc.

I have listed the above in order of priority, as I had found out years ago (through almost flunking my freshman year in engineering) that if you didn't use priorities, when the music stopped you were left standing. Some of these priorities ran concurrently, of course; I expected to search out Ricky and probably Belle & Co. as well, while I was boning engineering. But first things first and second things second; finding a job came even ahead of hunting for a sack because dollars are the key to everything else . . . when you haven't got them.

After getting turned down six times in town I had chased an ad clear out to San Bernardino Borough, only to get there ten minutes too late. I should have rented a flop at once; instead I played it real smart and went back downtown, intending to find a room, then get up very early and be first in line for some job listed in the early edition.

How was I to know? I got my name on four rooming-house waiting lists and wound up in the park. I stayed there, walking to keep warm, until almost midnight, then gave up—Great Los Angeles winters are subtropical only if you accent the "sub." I then took refuge in a station of Wilshire Ways . . . and about two in the morning they rounded me up with the rest of the vagrants.

Jails have improved. This one was warm and I think they required the cockroaches to wipe their feet.

I was charged with barracking. The judge was a young fellow who didn't even look up from his newspaper but simply said, "These all first offenders?"

"Yes, your honor."

"Thirty days, or take a labor-company parole. Next."

They started to march us out but I didn't budge. "Just a minute, Judge."

"Eh? Something troubling you? Are you guilty or not guilty?"

"Uh, I really don't know because I don't know what it is I have done. You see——"

"Do you want a public defender? If you do you can be locked up until one can handle your case. I understand they are running about six days late right now . . . but it's your privilege."

"Uh, I still don't know. Maybe what I want is a labor-company parole, though I'm not sure what it is. What I really want is some advice from the Court, if the Court pleases."

The judge said to the bailiff, "Take the others out." He turned back to me. "Spill it. But I'll warrant you won't like my advice. I've been on this job long enough to have heard every phony story and to have acquired a deep disgust toward most of them."

"Yes, sir. Mine isn't phony; it's easily checked. You see, I just got out of the Long Sleep yesterday and——"

But he did look disgusted. "One of those, eh? I've often wondered what made our grandparents think they could dump their riffraff on us. The last thing on earth this city needs is more people . . . especially ones who couldn't get along in their own time. I wish I could boot you back to whatever year you came from with a message to everybody there that the future they're dreaming about is not, repeat *not*, paved with gold." He sighed. "But it wouldn't do any good, I'm sure. Well, what do you expect me to do? Give you another chance? Then have you pop up here again a week from now?"

"Judge, I don't think I'm likely to. I've got enough money to live until I find a job and——"

"Eh? If you've got money, what were you doing barracking?"

"Judge, I don't even know what that word means." This time he let me explain. When I came to how I had been swindled by Master Insurance Company his whole manner changed.

"Those swine! My mother got taken by them after she had paid premiums for twenty years. Why didn't you tell me this in the first place?" He took out a card, wrote something on it, and said, "Take this to the hiring office at the Surplus & Salvage Authority. If you don't get a job come back and see me this afternoon. But no more barracking. Not only does it breed crime and vice, but you yourself are running a terrible risk of meeting up with a zombie recruiter."

That's how I got a job smashing up brand-new ground cars. But I still think I made no mistake in logic in deciding to job-hunt first. Anywhere is home to the man with a fat bank account —the cops leave him alone.

I found a decent room, too, within my budget, in a part of West Los Angeles which had not yet been changed over to New Plan. I think it had formerly been a coat closet.

I would not want anyone to think I disliked the year 2000, as compared with 1970. I liked it and I liked 2001 when it rolled around a couple of weeks after they wakened me. In spite of recurrent spasms of almost unbearable homesickness, I thought that Great Los Angeles at the dawn of the Third Millennium was odds-on the most wonderful place I had ever seen. It was fast and clean and very exciting, even if it was too crowded . . . and even that was being coped with on a mammoth, venturesome scale. The New Plan parts of town were a joy to an engineer's heart. If the city government had had the sovereign power to stop immigration for ten years, they could have licked the housing problem. Since they did not have that power, they just had to do their best with the swarms that kept rolling over the Sierras—and their best was spectacular beyond belief and even the failures were colossal.

It was worth sleeping thirty years just to wake up in a time when they had licked the common cold and nobody had a post-nasal drip. That meant more to me than the research colony on Venus.

Two things impressed me most, one big, one little. The big one was NullGrav, of course. Back in 1970 I had known about the Babson Institute gravitation research but I had not expected anything to come of it—and nothing had; the basic field theory on which NullGrav is based was developed at the University of Edinburgh. But I had been taught in school that gravitation was something that nobody could ever do anything about, because it was inherent in the very shape of space.

So they changed the shape of space, naturally. Only temporarily and locally, to be sure, but that's all that's needed in moving a heavy object. It still has to stay in field relation with Mother Terra, so it's useless for space ships—or it is in 2001; I've quit making bets about the future. I learned that to make a lift it was still necessary to expend power to overcome the gravity potential, and conversely, to lower something you had to have a power pack to store all those foot-pounds in, or something would go Phzzt!-*Spung!* But just to transport something horizontally, say from San Francisco to Great Los Angeles, just lift it once, then float along, no power at all, like an ice skater riding a long edge.

Lovely!

I tried to study the theory of it, but the math starts in where tensor calculus leaves off; it's not for me. But an engineer is rarely a mathematical physicist and he does not have to be; he simply has to savvy the skinny of a thing well enough to know what it can do in practical applications—know the working parameters. I could learn those.

The "little thing" I mentioned was the changes in female styles made possible by the Sticktite fabrics. I was not startled by mere skin on bathing beaches; you could see that coming in 1970. But the weird things that the ladies could do with Sticktite made my jaw sag.

My grandpappy was born in 1890; I suppose that some of the sights in 1970 would have affected him the same way.

But I liked the fast new world and would have been happy in it if I had not been so bitterly lonely so much of the time. I was out of joint. There were times (in the middle of the night, usually) when I would gladly have swapped it all for one beat-up tomcat, or for a chance to spend an afternoon taking little Ricky to the zoo . . . or for the comradeship Miles and I had shared when all we had was hard work and hope.

It was still early in 2001 and I wasn't halfway caught up on my homework, when I began to itch to leave my feather-bedded job and get back to the old drawing board. There were so many, many things possible under current art which had been impossible in 1970; I wanted to get busy and design a few dozen.

For example I had expected that there would be automatic secretaries in use—I mean a machine you could dictate to and get back a business letter, spelling, punctuation, and format all perfect, without a human being in the sequence. But there weren't any. Oh, somebody had invented a machine which could type, but it was suited only to a phonetic language like Esperanto and was useless in a language in which you could say: "Though the tough cough and hiccough plough him through."

People won't give up the illogicalities of English to suit the convenience of an inventor. Mohammed must go to the mountain.

If a high-school girl could sort out the cockeyed spelling of English and usually type the right word, how could a machine be taught to do it?

"Impossible" was the usual answer. It was supposed to require human judgment and understanding.

But an invention is something that was "impossible" up to then —that's why governments grant patents.

With memory tubes and the miniaturization now possible— I had been right about the importance of gold as an engineering material—with those two things it would be easy to pack a hundred thousand sound codes into a cubic foot . . . in other words, to sound-key every word in a Webster's Collegiate Dictionary. But that was unnecessary; ten thousand would be ample. Who expects a stenographer to field a word like "kourbash" or "pyrophyllite"? You spell such words for her if you must use them. Okay, we code the machine to accept spelling when necessary. We sound-code for punctuation . . . and for various formats . . . and to look up addresses in a file . . . and for how many copies . . . and routing . . . and provide at least a thousand blank word-codings for special vocabulary used in a business or profession— and make it so that the owner-client could put those special words in himself, spell a word like "stenobenthic" with the memory key depressed and never have to spell it again.

All simple. Just a matter of hooking together gadgets already on the market, then smoothing it into a production model.

The real hitch was homonyms. *Dictation Daisy* wouldn't even slow up over that "tough cough and hiccough" sentence because each of those words carry a different sound. But choices like "they're" and "their," "right" and "write" would give her trouble.

Did the L. A. Public Library have a dictionary of English homonyms? It did . . . and I began counting the unavoidable homonym pairs and trying to figure how many of these could be handled by information theory through context statistics and how many would require special coding.

I began to get jittery with frustration. Not only was I wasting thirty hours a week on an utterly useless job, but also I could not do real engineering in a public library. I needed a drafting room, a shop where I could smooth out the bugs, trade catalogues, professional journals, calculating machines, and all the rest.

I decided that I would just have to get at least a subprofessional job. I wasn't silly enough to think that I was an engineer again; there was too much art I had not yet soaked up—repeatedly I had thought of ways to do something, using something new that I had learned, only to find out at the library that somebody had solved the same problem, neater, better, and cheaper than my own first stab at it and ten or fifteen years earlier.

I needed to get into an engineering office and let these new things soak in through my skin. I had hopes that I could land a job as a junior draftsman.

I knew that they were using powered semi-automatic drafting machines now; I had seen pictures of them even though I had not had one under my hands. But I had a hunch that I could learn to play one in twenty minutes, given the chance, for they were remarkably like an idea I had once had myself: a machine that bore the same relation to the old-fashioned drawing-board-and-T-square method that a typewriter did to writing in longhand. I had worked it all out in my head, how you could put straight lines or curves anywhere on an easel just by punching keys.

However, in this case I was just as sure that my idea had not been stolen as I was certain that *Flexible Frank* had been stolen, because my drafting machine had never existed except in my head. Somebody had had the same idea and had developed it logically the same way. When it's time to railroad, people start railroading.

The Aladdin people, the same firm that made *Eager Beaver*, made one of the best drawing machines, *Drafting Dan*. I dipped into my savings, bought a better suit of clothes and a second-hand brief case, stuffed the latter with newspapers, and presented myself at the Aladdin salesrooms with a view to "buying" one. I asked for a demonstration.

Then, when I got close to a model of *Drafting Dan*, I had a most upsetting experience. *Déjà vu*, the psychologists call it—"I have been here before." The damned thing had been developed in precisely the fashion in which I would have developed it, had I had time to do so . . . instead of being kidnaped into the Long Sleep.

Don't ask me exactly why I felt that way. A man knows his own style of work. An art critic will say that a painting is a Rubens or a Rembrandt by the brushwork, the treatment of light, the composition, the choice of pigment, a dozen things. Engineering is not science, it is an art, and there is always a wide range of choices in how to solve engineering problems. An engineering designer "signs" his work by those choices just as surely as a painter does.

Drafting Dan had the flavor of my own technique so strongly that I was quite disturbed by it. I began to wonder if there wasn't something to telepathy after all.

I was careful to get the number of its first patent. In the state I was in I wasn't surprised to see that the date on the first one was 1970. I resolved to find out who had invented it. It might have been one of my own teachers, from whom I had picked up some of my style. Or it might be an engineer with whom I had once worked.

The inventor might still be alive. If so, I'd look him up some-day . . . get acquainted with this man whose mind worked just like mine.

But I managed to pull myself together and let the salesman show me how to work it. He hardly need have bothered; *Drafting Dan* and I were made for each other. In ten minutes I could play it better than he could. At last I reluctantly quit making pretty pictures with it, got list price, discounts, service arrangements, and so forth, then left saying that I would call him, just as he was ready to get my signature on the dotted line. It was a dirty trick, but all I cost him was an hour's time.

From there I went to the Hired Girl main factory and applied for a job.

I knew that Belle and Miles were no longer with Hired Girl, Inc. In what time I could spare between my job and the compelling necessity to catch up in engineering I had been searching for Belle and Miles and most especially for Ricky. None of the three was listed in the Great Los Angeles telephone system, nor for that matter anywhere in the United States, for I had paid to have an "information" search made at the national office in Cleveland. A quadruple fee, it was, as I had had Belle searched for under both "Gentry" and "Darkin."

I had the same luck with the Register of Voters for Los Angeles County.

Hired Girl, Inc., in a letter from a seventeenth vice-president in charge of foolish questions, admitted cautiously that they had once had officers by those names thirty years ago but they were unable to help me now.

Picking up a trail thirty years cold is no job for an amateur with little time and less money. I did not have their fingerprints, or I might have tried the FBI. I didn't know their social-security numbers. My Country 'Tis of Thee had never succumbed to police-state nonsense, so there was no bureau certain to have a dossier on each citizen, nor was I in a position to tap such a file even if there had been.

Perhaps a detective agency, lavishly subsidized, could have dug through utilities records, newspaper files, and God knows what, and traced them down. But I didn't have the lavish subsidy, nor the talent and time to do it myself.

I finally gave up on Miles and Belle while promising myself that I would, as quickly as I could afford it, put professionals to tracing Ricky. I had already determined that she held no Hired Girl stock and I had written to the Bank of America to see if they held, or ever had held, a trust for her. I got back a form letter informing me that such things were confidential, so I had written again, saying that I was a Sleeper and she was my only surviving relative. That time I got a nice letter, signed by one of the trust officers and saying that he regretted that information concerning trust beneficiaries could not be divulged even to one in my exceptional circumstances, but he felt justified in giving me the negative information that the bank had not at any time through any of its branches held a trust in favor of one Frederica Virginia Gentry.

That seemed to settle one thing. Somehow those birds had managed to get the stock away from little Ricky. My assignment of the stock would have had to go through the Bank of America, the way I had written it. But it had not. Poor Ricky! We had both been robbed.

I made one more stab at it. The records office of the Superintendent of Instruction in Mojave did have record of a grade-school pupil named Frederica Virginia Gentry . . . but the named pupil had taken a withdrawal transcript in 1971. Further deponent sayeth not.

It was some consolation to know that somebody somewhere admitted that Ricky had ever existed. But she might have taken that transcript to any of many, many thousand public schools in the United States. How long would it take to write to each of them? And were their records so arranged as to permit them to answer, even supposing they were willing?

In a quarter of a billion people one little girl can drop out of sight like a pebble in the ocean.

But the failure of my search did leave me free to seek a job with Hired Girl, Inc., now that I knew Miles and Belle were not running it. I could have tried any of a hundred automation firms, but Hired Girl and Aladdin were the big names in appliance automatons, as important in their own field as Ford and General Motors had been in the heyday of the ground automobile. I picked Hired Girl partly for sentimental reasons; I wanted to see what my old outfit had grown into.

On Monday, 5 March, 2001, I went to their employment office, got into the line for white-collar help, filled out a dozen forms having nothing to do with engineering and one that did . . . and was told don't-call-us-we'll-call-you.

I hung around and managed to bull myself in to see an assistant hiring flunky. He reluctantly looked over the one form that meant anything and told me that my engineering degree meant nothing, since there had been a thirty-year lapse when I had not used my skill.

I pointed out that I had been a Sleeper.

"That makes it even worse. In any case, we don't hire people over forty-five."

"But I'm *not* forty-five. I'm only thirty."

"You were born in 1940. Sorry."

"What am I supposed to do? Shoot myself?"

He shrugged. "If I were you, I'd apply for an old-age pension."

I got out quickly before I gave him some advice. Then I walked three quarters of a mile around to the front entrance and went in. The general manager's name was Curtis; I asked for him.

I got past the first two layers simply by insisting that I had business with him. Hired Girl, Inc., did not use their own automatons as receptionists; they used real flesh and blood. Eventually I reached a place several stories up and (I judged) about two doors from the boss, and here I encountered a firm pass-gauge type who insisted on knowing my business.

I looked around. It was a largish office with about forty real people in it, as well as a lot of machines. She said sharply, "Well? State your business and I'll check with Mr. Curtis's appointment secretary."

I said loudly, making sure that everybody heard it, "I want to know what he's going to do about my wife!"

Sixty seconds later I was in his private office. He looked up. "Well? What the devil is this nonsense?"

It took half an hour and some old records to convince him that I did not have a wife and that I actually was the founder of the firm. Then things got chummy over drinks and cigars and I met the sales manager and the chief engineer and other heads of departments. "We thought you were dead," Curtis told me. "In fact, the company's official history says that you are."

"Just a rumor. Some other D. B. Davis."

The sales manager, Jack Galloway, said suddenly, "What are you doing now, Mr. Davis?"

"Not much. I've, uh, been in the automobile business. But I'm resigning. Why?"

" 'Why?' Isn't it obvious?" He swung around toward the chief engineer, Mr. McBee. "Hear that, Mac? All you engineers are alike; you wouldn't know a sales angle if it came up and kissed you. 'Why?' Mr. Davis. Because you're sales copy, that's why! Because you're romance. Founder of Firm Comes Back from Grave to Visit Brain Child. Inventor of the First Robot Servant Views Fruits of His Genius."

I said hastily, "Now wait a minute—I'm not an advertising model nor a grabbie star. I like my privacy. I didn't come here for that; I came here for a job . . . in engineering."

Mr. McBee's eyebrows went up but he said nothing.

We wrangled for a while. Galloway tried to tell me that it was my simple duty to the firm I had founded. McBee said little, but it was obvious that he did not think I would be any addition to his department—at one point he asked me what I knew about designing solid circuits. I had to admit that my only knowledge of them was from a little reading of non-classified publications.

Curtis finally suggested a compromise. "See here, Mr. Davis, you obviously occupy a very special position. One might say that you founded not merely this firm but the whole industry. Nevertheless, as Mr. McBee has hinted, the industry has moved on since the year you took the Long Sleep. Suppose we put you on the staff with the title of . . . uh, 'Research Engineer Emeritus.' "

I hesitated. "What would that mean?"

"Whatever you made it mean. However, I tell you frankly that you would be expected to co-operate with Mr. Galloway. We not only make these things, we have to sell them."

"Uh, would I have a chance to do any engineering?"

"That's up to you. You'd have facilities and you could do what you wished."

"Shop facilities?"

Curtis looked at McBee. The chief engineer answered, "Certainly, certainly . . . within reason, of course." He had slipped so far into Glasgow speech that I could hardly understand him.

Galloway said briskly. "That's settled. May I be excused, B.J.? Don't go away, Mr. Davis—we're going to get a picture of you with the very first model of *Hired Girl.*"

And he did. I was glad to see her . . . the very model I had put together with my own pinkies and lots of sweat. I wanted to see if she still worked, but McBee wouldn't let me start her up—I don't think he really believed that I knew how she worked.

I had a good time at Hired Girl all through March and April. I had all the professional tools I could want, technical journals, the indispensable trade catalogues, a practical library, a *Drafting Dan* (Hired Girl did not make a drafting machine themselves, so they used the best on the market, which was Aladdin's), and the shoptalk of professionals . . . music to my ears!

I got acquainted especially with Chuck Freudenberg, components assistant chief engineer. For my money Chuck was the only real engineer there; the rest were overeducated slipstick mechanics . . . including McBee, for the chief engineer was, I thought, a clear proof that it took more than a degree and a Scottish accent to make an engineer. After we got better acquainted Chuck admitted that he felt the same way. "Mac doesn't really like anything new; he would rather do things the way his grandpa did on the bonnie banks of the Clyde."

"What's he doing in this job?"

Freudenberg did not know the details, but it seemed that the present firm had been a manufacturing company which had simply rented the patents (my patents) from Hired Girl, Inc. Then about twenty years ago there had been one of those tax-saving mergers, with Hired Girl stock swapped for stock in the manufacturing firm and the new firm taking the name of the one I had founded. Chuck thought that McBee had been hired at that time. "He's got a piece of it, I think."

Chuck and I used to sit over beers in the evening and discuss engineering, what the company needed, and the whichness of what. His original interest in me had been that I was a Sleeper. Too many people, I had found, had a queezy interest in Sleepers (as if we were freaks) and I avoided letting people know that I was one. But Chuck was fascinated by the time jump itself and his interest was a healthy one in what the world had been like before he was born, as recalled by a man who literally remembered it as "only yesterday."

In return he was willing to criticize the new gadgets that

were always boiling up in my head, and set me straight when I (as I did repeatedly) would rough out something that was old hat . . . in 2001 A.D. Under his friendly guidance I was becoming a modern engineer, catching up fast.

But when I outlined to him one April evening my autosecretary idea he said slowly, "Dan, have you done work on this on company time?"

"Huh? No, not really. Why?"

"How does your contract read?"

"What? I don't have one." Curtis had put me on the payroll and Galloway had taken pictures of me and had a ghost writer asking me silly questions; that was all.

"Mmm . . . pal, I wouldn't do anything about this until you are sure where you stand. This is really new. And I think you can make it work."

"I hadn't worried about that angle."

"Put it away for a while. You know the shape the company is in. It's making money and we put out good products. But the only new items we've brought out in five years are ones we've acquired by license. *I* can't get anything new past Mac. But you can by-pass Mac and take this to the big boss. So don't . . . unless you want to hand it over to the company just for your salary check."

I took his advice. I continued to design but I burned any drawings I thought were good—I didn't need them once I had them in my head. I didn't feel guilty about it; they hadn't hired me as an engineer, they were paying me to be a show-window dummy for Galloway. When my advertising value was sucked dry, they would give me a month's pay and a vote of thanks and let me go.

But by then I'd be a real engineer again and able to open my own office. If Chuck wanted to take a flyer I'd take him with me.

Instead of handing my story to the newspapers Jack Galloway played it slow for the national magazines; he wanted *Life* to do a spread, tying it in with the one they had done a third of a century earlier on the first production model of *Hired Girl*. *Life* did not rise to the bait but he did manage to plant it several other places that spring, tying it in with display advertising.

I thought of growing a beard. Then I realized that no one recognized me and would not have cared if they had.

I got a certain amount of crank mail, including one letter from a man who promised me that I would burn eternally in hell for defying God's plan for my life. I chucked it, while thinking that if God had really opposed what had happened to me, He should never have made cold sleep possible. Otherwise I wasn't bothered.

But I did get a phone call, on Thursday, 3 May, 2001. "Mrs. Schultz is on the line, sir. Will you take the call?"

Schultz? Damnation, I had promised Doughty the last time I had called him that I would take care of that. But I had put it off because I did not want to; I was almost sure it was one of those screwballs who pursued Sleepers and asked them personal questions.

But she had called several times, Doughty had told me, since I had checked out in December. In accordance with the policy of the sanctuary they had refused to give her my address, agreeing merely to pass along messages.

Well, I owed it to Doughty to shut her up. "Put her on."

"Is this Danny Davis?" My office phone had no screen; she could not see me.

"Speaking. Your name is Schultz?"

"Oh, Danny darling, it's so *good* to hear your voice!"

I didn't answer right away. She went on, "Don't you *know* me?"

I knew her, all right. It was Belle Gentry.

VII

I made a date with her.

My first impulse had been to tell her to go to hell and switch off. I had long since realized that revenge was childish; revenge would not bring Pete back and fitting revenge would simply land me in jail. I had hardly thought about Belle and Miles since I had quit looking for them.

But Belle almost certainly knew where Ricky was. So I made a date.

She wanted me to take her to dinner, but I would not do that. I'm not fussy about fine points of etiquette. But eating is something you do only with friends; I would see her but I had no intention of eating or drinking with her. I got her address and told her I would be there that evening at eight.

It was a cheap rental, a walk-up flat in a part of town (lower La Brea) not yet converted to New Plan. Before I buzzed her door I knew that she had not hung onto what she had bilked me out of, or she would not have been living there.

And when I saw her I realized that revenge was much too late; she and the years had managed it for me.

Belle was not less than fifty-three by the age she had claimed, and probably closer to sixty in fact. Between geriatrics and endocrinology a woman who cared to take the trouble could stay looking thirty for at least thirty extra years, and lots of them did. There were grabbie stars who boasted of being grandmothers while still playing ingénue leads.

Belle had not taken the trouble.

She was fat and shrill and kittenish. It was evident that she still considered her body her principal asset, for she was dressed in a Sticktite negligee which, while showing much too much of her, also showed that she was female, mammalian, overfed, and underexercised.

She was not aware of it. That once-keen brain was fuzzy; all that was left was her conceit and her overpowering confidence in herself. She threw herself on me with squeals of joy and came close to kissing me before I could unwind her.

I pushed her wrists back. "Take it easy, Belle."

"But, darling! I'm so happy—so excited—and so *thrilled* to see you!"

"I'll bet." I had gone there resolved to keep my temper . . . just find out what I wanted to know and get out. But I was finding it difficult. "Remember how you saw me last? Drugged to my eyebrows so that you could stuff me into cold sleep."

She looked puzzled and hurt. "But, sweetheart, we only did it for your own good! You were *so* ill."

I think she believed it. "Okay, okay. Where's Miles? You're Mrs. Schultz now?"

Her eyes grew wide. "Didn't you *know?*"

"Know what?"

"Poor Miles . . . poor, *dear* Miles. He lived less than two years, Danny boy, after you left us." Her expression changed suddenly. "The frallup cheated me!"

"That's too bad." I wondered how he had died. Did he fall or was he pushed? Arsenic soup? I decided to stick to the main issue before she jumped the track completely. "What became of Ricky?"

"Ricky?"

"Miles's little girl. Frederica."

"Oh, that horrible little brat! How should I know? She went to live with her grandmother."

"Where? And what was her grandmother's name?"

"Where? Tucson—or Yuma—or some place dull like that. It

112

might have been Indio. Darling, I don't want to talk about that impossible child—I want to talk about *us*."

"In a moment. What was her grandmother's name?"

"Danny boy, you're being very tiresome. Why in the world should I remember something like that?"

"What was it?"

"Oh, Hanolon . . . or Haney . . . or Heinz. Or it might have been Hinckley. Don't be dull, dear. Let's have a drink. Let's drink a toast to our happy reunion."

I shook my head. "I don't use the stuff." This was almost true. Having discovered that it was an unreliable friend in a crisis, I usually limited myself to a beer with Chuck Freudenberg.

"How very dull, dearest. You won't mind if I have one." She was already pouring it—straight gin, the lonely girl's friend. But before she downed it she picked up a plastic pill bottle and rolled two capsules into her palm. "Have one?"

I recognized the striped casing—euphorion. It was supposed to be non-toxic and non-habit-forming, but opinions differed. There was agitation to class it with morphine and the barbiturates. "Thanks. I'm happy now."

"How nice." She took both of them, chased them with gin. I decided if I was to learn anything at all I had better talk fast; soon she would be nothing but giggles.

I took her arm and sat her down on her couch, then sat down across from her. "Belle, tell me about yourself. Bring me up to date. How did you and Miles make out with the Mannix people?"

"Uh? But we didn't." She suddenly flared up. "That was *your* fault!"

"Huh? My fault? I wasn't even there."

"Of course it was your fault. That monstrous thing you built out of an old wheel chair . . . *that* was what they wanted. And then it was gone."

"Gone? Where was it?"

She peered at me with piggy, suspicious eyes. "You ought to know. You took it."

"Me? Belle, are you crazy? I couldn't take anything. I was frozen stiff, in cold sleep. Where was it? And when did it disappear?" It fitted in with my own notions that somebody must have swiped *Flexible Frank,* if Belle and Miles had not made use of him. But out of all the billions on the globe, I was the one who certainly had not. I had not seen *Frank* since that disastrous night when they had outvoted me. "Tell me about it, Belle. Where was it? And what made you think *I* took it?"

"It had to be you. Nobody else knew it was important. That pile of junk! I *told* Miles not to put it in the garage."

"But if somebody did swipe it, I doubt if they could make it work. You still had all the notes and instructions and drawings."

"No, we didn't either. Miles, the fool, had stuffed them all inside it the night we had to move it to protect it."

I did not fuss about the word "protect." Instead I was about to say that he couldn't possibly have stuffed several pounds of paper into *Flexible Frank;* he was already stuffed like a goose—when I remembered that I had built a temporary shelf across the bottom of his wheel-chair base to hold tools while I worked on him. A man in a hurry might very well have emptied my working files into that space.

No matter. The crime, or crimes, had been committed thirty years ago. I wanted to find out how Hired Girl, Inc., had slipped away from them. "After the Mannix deal fell through what did you do with the company?"

"We ran it, of course. Then when Jake quit us Miles said we had to shut down. Miles was a weakling . . . and I never liked that Jake Schmidt. Sneaky. Always asking why you had quit . . . as if we could have stopped you! I wanted us to hire a *good* foreman and keep going. The company would have been worth more. But Miles insisted."

"What happened then?"

"Why, then we licensed to Geary Manufacturing, of course. You know that; you're working there now."

I did know that; the full corporate name of Hired Girl was now "Hired Girl Appliances and Geary Manufacturing, Inc." —even though the signs read simply "Hired Girl." I seemed to have found out all I needed to know that this flabby old wreck could tell me.

But I was curious on another point. "You two sold your stock after you licensed to Geary?"

"Huh? Whatever put that silly notion in your head?" Her expression broke and she began to blubber, pawing feebly for a handkerchief, then giving up and letting the tears go. "He cheated me! He cheated me! The dirty shiker *cheated* me . . . he kinked me out of it." She snuffled and added meditatively, "You all cheated me . . . and you were the worst of the lot, Danny boy. After I had been so good to you." She started to bawl again.

I decided that euphorion wasn't worth whatever it cost. Or maybe she enjoyed crying. "How did he cheat you, Belle?"

"What? Why, *you* know. He left it all to that dirty brat of his . . . after all that he had promised me . . . after I nursed him when he hurt so. And she *wasn't even his own daughter*. That proves it."

It was the first good news I had had all evening. Apparently Ricky had received one good break, even if they had grabbed my stock away from her earlier. So I got back to the main point. "Belle, what was Ricky's grandmother's name? And where did they live?"

"Where did *who* live?"

"Ricky's grandmother."

"Who's Ricky?"

"Miles's daughter. Try to think, Belle. It's important."

That set her off. She pointed a finger at me and shrilled, "I know *you*. You were in *love* with her, that's what. That dirty little sneak . . . her and that horrible cat."

I felt a burst of anger at the mention of Pete. But I tried to suppress it. I simply grabbed her shoulders and shook her a little. "Brace up, Belle. I want to know just one thing. Where did they live? How did Miles address letters when he wrote to them?"

She kicked at me. "I won't even talk to you! You've been perfectly stinking ever since you got here." Then she appeared to sober almost instantly and said quietly, "I don't know. The grandmother's name was Haneker, or something like that. I only saw her once, in court, when they came to see about the will."

"When was that?"

"Right after Miles died, of course."

"When did Miles die, Belle?"

She switched again. "You want to know too much. You're as bad as the sheriffs . . . questions, questions, questions!" Then she looked up and said pleadingly, "Let's forget everything and just be ourselves. There's just you and me now, dear . . . and we still

have our lives ahead of us. A woman isn't old at thirty-nine . . .
Schultzie said I was the youngest thing he ever saw—and that old
goat had seen plenty, let me tell you! We could be so happy,
dear. We——"

I had had all I could stand, even to play detective. "I've got
to go, Belle."

"What, dear? Why, it's early . . . and we've got all night ahead
of us. I thought——"

"I don't care what you thought. I've got to leave right now."

"Oh dear! Such a pity. When will I see you again? Tomorrow?
I'm terribly busy but I'll break my engagements and——"

"I won't be seeing you again, Belle." I left.

I never did see her again.

As soon as I was home I took a hot bath, scrubbing hard. Then
I sat down and tried to add up what I had found out, if anything.
Belle seemed to think that Ricky's grandmother's name began
with an "H"—if Belle's maunderings meant anything at all, a matter highly doubtful—and that they had lived in one of the desert
towns in Arizona, or possibly California. Well, perhaps professional skip-tracers could make something of that.

Or maybe not. In any case it would be tedious and expensive;
I'd have to wait until I could afford it.

Did I know anything else that signified?

Miles had died (so Belle said) around 1972. If he had died
in this county I ought to be able to find the date in a couple of
hours of searching, and after that I ought to be able to track down
the hearing on his will . . . if there had been one, as Belle had
implied. Through that I might be able to find out where Ricky
had lived then. If courts kept such records. (I didn't know.) If I
had gained anything by cutting the lapse down to twenty-eight
years and locating the town she had lived in that long ago.

If there was any point in looking for a woman now forty-one
and almost certainly married and with a family. The jumbled
ruin that had once been Belle Darkin had shaken me; I was beginning to realize what thirty years could mean. Not that I feared
that Ricky grown up would be anything but gracious and good
. . . but would she even remember me? Oh, I did not think she
would have forgotten me entirely, but wasn't it likely that I would

be just a faceless person, the man she had sometimes called "Uncle Danny" and who had that nice cat?

Wasn't I, in my own way, living in a fantasy of the past quite as much as Belle was?

Oh well, it couldn't hurt to try again to find her. At the least, we could exchange Christmas cards each year. Her husband could not very well object to that.

VIII

The next morning was Friday, the fourth of May. Instead of going into the office I went down to the county Hall of Records. They were moving everything and told me to come back next month, so I went to the office of the *Times* and got a crick in my neck from a microscanner. But I did find out that if Miles had died any date between twelve and thirty-six months after I had been tucked in the freezer, he had not done so in Los Angeles County—if the death notices were correct.

Of course there was no law requiring him to die in L. A. County. You can die anyplace. They've never managed to regulate that.

Perhaps Sacramento had consolidated state records. I decided I would have to check someday, thanked the *Times* librarian, went out to lunch, and eventually got back to Hired Girl, Inc.

There were two phone calls and a note waiting, all from Belle. I got as far in the note as "Dearest Dan," tore it up and told the desk not to accept any calls for me from Mrs. Schultz. Then I went over to the accounting office and asked the chief accountant if there was any way to check up on past ownership of a retired stock issue. He said he would try and I gave him the numbers, from memory, of the original Hired Girl stock I had once held. It took no feat of memory; we had issued exactly one thousand shares to start with and I had held the first five hundred and ten, and Belle's "engagement present" had come off the front end.

I went back to my cubbyhole and found McBee waiting for me.

"Where have you been?" he wanted to know.

"Out and around. Why?"

"That's hardly a sufficient answer. Mr. Galloway was in twice today looking for you. I was forced to tell him I did not know where you were."

"Oh, for Pete's sake! If Galloway wants me he'll find me eventually. If he spent half the time peddling the merchandise on its merits that he does trying to think up cute new angles, the firm would be better off." Galloway was beginning to annoy me. He was supposed to be in charge of selling, but it seemed to me that he concentrated on kibitzing the advertising agency that handled our account. But I'm prejudiced; engineering is the only part that interests me. All the rest strikes me as paper shuffling, mere overhead.

I knew what Galloway wanted me for and, to tell the truth, I had been dragging my feet. He wanted to dress me up in 1900 costumes and take pictures. I had told him that he could take all the pix he wanted of me in 1970 costumes, but that 1900 was twelve years before my father was born. He said nobody would know the difference, so I told him what the fortuneteller told the cop. He said I didn't have the right attitude.

These people who deal in fancification to fool the public think nobody can read and write but themselves.

McBee said, "You don't have the right attitude, Mr. Davis."

"So? I'm sorry."

"You're in an odd position. You are charged to my department, but I'm supposed to make you available to advertising and sales when they need you. From here on I think you had better use the time clock like everyone else . . . and you had better check with me whenever you leave the office during working hours. Please see to it."

I counted to ten slowly, using binary notation. "Mac, do *you* use the time clock?"

"Eh? Of course not. I'm the chief engineer."

"So you are. It says so right over on that door. But see here,

Mac, I was chief engineer of this bolt bin before you started to shave. Do you really think that I am going to knuckle under to a time clock?"

He turned red. "Possibly not. But I can tell you this: if you don't, you won't draw your check."

"So? You didn't hire me; you can't fire me."

"Mmm . . . we'll see. I can at least transfer you out of my department and over to advertising where you belong. If you belong anywhere." He glanced at my drafting machine. "You certainly aren't producing anything here. I don't fancy having that expensive machine tied up any longer." He nodded briskly. "Good day."

I followed him out. An *Office Boy* rolled in and placed a large envelope in my basket, but I did not wait to see what it was; I went down to the staff coffee bar and fumed. Like a lot of other triple-ought-gauge minds, Mac thought creative work could be done by the numbers. No wonder the old firm hadn't produced anything new for years.

Well, to hell with him. I hadn't planned to stick around much longer anyway.

An hour or so later I wandered back up and found an interoffice mail envelope in my basket. I opened it, thinking that Mac had decided to throw the switch on me at once.

But it was from accounting; it read:

Dear Mr. Davis:
Re: the stock you inquired about.
Dividends on the larger block were paid from first quarter 1971 to second quarter 1980 on the original shares, to a trust held in favor of a party named Heinicke. Our reorganization took place in 1980 and the abstract at hand is somewhat obscure, but it appears that the equivalent shares (after reorganization) were sold to Cosmopolitan Insurance Group, which still holds them. Regarding the smaller block of stock, it was held (as you suggested) by Belle D. Gentry until 1972, when it was assigned to Sierra Acceptances Corporation, who broke it up and sold it piecemeal "over the counter." The exact subsequent history of each share and its equivalent after reorganization could be traced if needed, but more time would be required.

If this department can be of any further assistance to you, please feel free to call on us.

Y. E. Reuther, Ch. Acct.

I called Reuther and thanked him and told him that I had all I wanted. I knew now that my assignment to Ricky had never been effective. Since the transfer of my stock that did show in the record was clearly fraudulent, the deal whiffed of Belle; this third party could have been either another of her stooges or possibly a fictitious person—she was probably already planning on swindling Miles by then.

Apparently she had been short of cash after Miles's death and had sold off the smaller block. But I did not care what had happened to any of the stock once it passed out of Belle's control. I had forgotten to ask Reuther to trace Miles's stock . . . that might give a lead to Ricky even though she no longer held it. But it was late Friday already; I'd ask him Monday. Right now I wanted to open the large envelope still waiting for me, for I had spotted the return address.

I had written to the patent office early in March about the original patents on both *Eager Beaver* and *Drafting Dan*. My conviction that the original *Eager Beaver* was just another name for *Flexible Frank* had been somewhat shaken by my first upsetting experience with *Drafting Dan*; I had considered the possibility that the same unknown genius who had conceived *Dan* so nearly as I had imagined him might also have developed a parallel equivalent of *Flexible Frank*. The theory was bulwarked by the fact that both patents had been taken out the same year and both patents were held (or had been held until they expired) by the same company, Aladdin.

But I had to know. And if this inventor was still alive I wanted to meet him. He could teach me a thing or four.

I had written first to the patent office, only to get a form letter back that all records of expired patents were now kept in the National Archives in Carlsbad Caverns. So I wrote the Archives and got another form letter with a schedule of fees. So I wrote a third time, sending a postal order (no personal checks, please) for prints of the whole works on both patents—descriptions, claims, drawings, histories.

This fat envelope looked like my answer.

The one on top was 4,307,909, the basic for *Eager Beaver*. I turned to the drawings, ignoring for the moment both description and claims. Claims aren't important anyway except in court; the basic notion in writing up claims on an application for patent is to claim the whole wide world in the broadest possible terms, then let the patent examiners chew you down—this is why patent attorneys are born. The descriptions, on the other hand, have to be factual, but I can read drawings faster than I can read descriptions.

I had to admit that it did not look too much like *Flexible Frank*. It was better than *Flexible Frank;* it could do more and some of the linkages were simpler. The basic notion was the same—but that had to be true, as a machine controlled by Thorsen tubes and ancestral to *Eager Beaver* had to be based on the same principles I had used in *Flexible Frank*.

I could almost see myself developing just such a device . . . sort of a second-stage model of *Frank*. I had once had something of the sort in mind—*Frank* without *Frank's* household limitations.

I finally got around to looking up the inventor's name on the claims and description sheets.

I recognized it all right. It was D. B. Davis.

I looked at it while whistling "Time on My Hands" slowly and off key. So Belle had lied again. I wondered if there was any truth at all in that spate of drivel she had fed me. Of course Belle was a pathological liar, but I had read somewhere that pathological liars usually have a pattern, starting from the truth and embellishing it, rather than indulging in complete fancy. Quite evidently my model of *Frank* had never been "stolen" but had been turned over to some other engineer to smooth up, then the application had been made in my name.

But the Mannix deal had never gone through; that one fact was certain, since I knew it from company records. But Belle had said that their failure to produce *Flexible Frank* as contracted had soured the Mannix deal.

Had Miles grabbed *Frank* for himself, letting Belle think that it had been stolen? Or restolen, rather.

In that case . . . I dropped guessing at it, as hopeless, more hopeless than the search for Ricky. I might have to take a job with

Aladdin before I would be able to ferret out where they had gotten the basic patent and who had benefited by the deal. It probably was not worth it, since the patent was expired, Miles was dead, and Belle, if she had gained a dime out of it, had long since thrown it away. I had satisfied myself on the one point important to me, the thing I had set out to prove; i.e., that I myself was the original inventor. My professional pride was salved and who cares about money when three meals a day are taken care of? Not me.

So I turned to 4,307,910, the first *Drafting Dan*.

The drawings were a delight. I couldn't have planned it better myself; this boy really had it. I admired the economy of the linkages and the clever way the circuits had been used to reduce the moving parts to a minimum. Moving parts are like the vermiform appendix; a source of trouble to be done away with whenever possible.

He had even used an electric typewriter for his keyboard chassis, giving credit on the drawing to an IBM patent series. That was smart, that was engineering: never reinvent something that you can buy down the street.

I had to know who this brainy boy was, so I turned to the papers.

It was D. B. Davis.

After quite a long time I phoned Dr. Albrecht. They rounded him up and I told him who I was, since my office phone had no visual.

"I recognized your voice," he answered. "Hi there, son. How are you getting along with your new job?"

"Well enough. They haven't offered me a partnership yet."

"Give them time. Happy otherwise? Find yourself fitting back in?"

"Oh, sure! If I had known what a great place here and now is I'd have taken the Sleep earlier. You couldn't hire me to go back to 1970."

"Oh, come now! I remember that year pretty well. I was a kid then on a farm in Nebraska. I used to hunt and fish. I had fun. More than I have now."

"Well, to each his own. I like it now. But look, Doc, I didn't call up just to talk philosophy; I've got a little problem."

"Well, let's have it. It ought to be a relief; most people have big problems."

"Doc? Is it at all possible for the Long Sleep to cause amnesia?"

He hesitated before replying. "It is conceivably possible. I can't say that I've ever seen a case, as such. I mean unconnected with other causes."

"What are the things that cause amnesia?"

"Any number of things. The commonest, perhaps, is the patient's own subconscious wish. He forgets a sequence of events, or rearranges them, because the facts are unbearable to him. That's a functional amnesia in the raw. Then there is the old-fashioned knock on the head—amnesia from trauma. Or it might be amnesia through suggestion . . . under drugs or hypnosis. What's the matter, bub? Can't you find your checkbook?"

"It's not that. So far as I know, I'm getting along just fine now. But I can't get some things straight that happened before I took the Sleep . . . and it's got me worried."

"Mmm . . . any possibility of any of the causes I mentioned?"

"Yes," I said slowly. "Uh, all of them, except maybe the bump on the head . . . and even that might have happened while I was drunk."

"I neglected to mention," he said dryly, "the commonest temporary amnesia—pulling a blank while under the affluence of incohol. See here, son, why don't you come see me and we'll talk it over in detail? If I can't tag what is biting you—I'm not a psychiatrist, you know—I can turn you over to a hypno-analyst who will peel back your memory like an onion and tell you why you were late to school on the fourth of February your second-grade year. But he's pretty expensive, so why not give me a whirl first?"

I said, "Cripes, Doc, I've bothered you too much already . . . and you are pretty stuffy about taking money."

"Son, I'm always interested in my people; they're all the family I have."

So I put him off by saying that I would call him the first of the week if I wasn't straightened out. I wanted to think about it anyhow.

Most of the lights went out except in my office; a *Hired Girl*, scrubwoman type, looked in, twigged that the room was still occupied, and rolled silently away. I still sat there.

Presently Chuck Freudenberg stuck his head in and said, "I thought you left long ago. Wake up and finish your sleep at home."

I looked up. "Chuck, I've got a wonderful idea. Let's buy a barrel of beer and two straws."

He considered it carefully. "Well, it's Friday . . . and I always like to have a head on Monday; it lets me know what day it is."

"Carried and so ordered. Wait a second while I stuff some things in this brief case."

We had some beers, then we had some food, then we had more beers at a place where the music was good, then we moved on to another place where there was no music and the booths had hush linings and they didn't disturb you as long as you ordered something about once an hour. We talked. I showed him the patent records.

Chuck looked over the *Eager Beaver* prototype. "That's a real nice job, Dan. I'm proud of you, boy. I'd like your autograph."

"But look at this one." I gave him the drafting-machine patent papers.

"Some ways this one is even nicer. Dan, do you realize that you have probably had more influence on the present state of the art than, well, than Edison had in his period? You know that, boy?"

"Cut it out, Chuck; this is serious." I gestured abruptly at the pile of photostats. "Okay, so I'm responsible for one of them. But I *can't* be responsible for the other one. I didn't do it . . . unless I'm completely mixed up about my own life before I took the Sleep. Unless I've got amnesia."

"You've been saying that for the past twenty minutes. But you don't seem to have any open circuits. You're no crazier than is normal in an engineer."

I banged the table, making the steins dance. "I've got to *know!*"

"Steady there. So what are you going to do?"

"Huh?" I pondered it. "I'm going to pay a psychiatrist to dig it out of me."

He sighed. "I thought you might say that. Now look, Dan, let's suppose you pay this brain mechanic to do this and he reports that nothing is wrong, your memory is in fine shape, and all your relays are closed. What then?"

"That's impossible."

"That's what they told Columbus. You haven't even mentioned the most likely explanation."

"Huh? What?"

Without answering he signaled the waiter and told it to bring back the big phone book, extended area. I said, "What's the matter? You calling the wagon for me?"

"Not yet." He thumbed through the enormous book, then stopped and said, "Dan, scan this."

I looked. He had his finger on "Davis." There were columns of Davises. But where he had his finger there were a dozen "D. B. Davises"—from "Dabney" to "Duncan."

There were three "Daniel B. Davises." One of them was me.

"That's from less than seven million people," he pointed out. "Want to try your luck on more than two hundred and fifty million?"

"It doesn't prove anything," I said feebly.

"No," he agreed, "it doesn't. It would be quite a coincidence, I readily agree, if two engineers with such similar talents happened to be working on the same sort of thing at the same time and just happened to have the same last name and the same initials. By the laws of statistics we could probably approximate just how unlikely it is that it would happen. But people forget—especially those who ought to know better, such as yourself—that while the laws of statistics tell you how unlikely a particular coincidence is, they state just as firmly that coincidences *do happen*. This looks like one. I like that a lot better than I like the theory that my beer buddy has slipped his cams. Good beer buddies are hard to come by."

"What do you think I ought to do?"

"The first thing to do is not to waste your time and money on a psychiatrist until you try the second thing. The second thing is to find out the first name of this 'D. B. Davis' who filed this patent. There will be some easy way to do that. Likely as not his first name will be 'Dexter.' Or even 'Dorothy.' But don't trip a breaker if it is 'Daniel,' because the middle name might be 'Berzowski' with a social-security number different from yours. And the third thing to do, which is really the first, is to forget it for now and order another round."

So we did, and talked of other things, particularly women. Chuck had a theory that women were closely related to machinery, both utterly unpredictable by logic. He drew graphs on the table top in beer to prove his thesis.

Sometime later I said suddenly, "If there were real time travel, I know what I would do."

"Huh? What are you talking about?"

"About my problem. Look, Chuck, I got here—got to 'now' I mean—by a sort of half-baked, horse-and-buggy time travel. But the trouble is I can't go back. All the things that are worrying me happened thirty years ago. I'd go back and dig out the truth . . . if there were such a thing as real time travel."

He stared at me. "But there *is*."

"*What?*"

He suddenly sobered. "I shouldn't have said that."

I said, "Maybe not, but you already have said it. Now you'd better tell me what you meant before I empty this here stein over your head."

"Forget it, Dan. I made a slip."

"Talk!"

"That's just what I can't do." He glanced around. No one was near us. "It's classified."

"Time travel classified? Good God, *why?*"

"Hell, boy, didn't you ever work for the government? They'd classify sex if they could. There doesn't have to be a reason; it's just their *policy*. But it *is* classified and I'm bound by it. So lay off."

"But—— Quit fooling around about it, Chuck; this is important to me. Terribly important." When he didn't answer and looked stubborn I said, "You can tell *me*. Shucks, I used to have a 'Q' clearance myself. Never suspended, either. It's just that I'm no longer with the government."

"What's a 'Q' clearance?"

I explained and presently he nodded. "You mean an 'Alpha' status. You must have been hot stuff, boy; I only rated a 'Beta.'"

"Then why can't you tell me?"

"Huh? You know why. Regardless of your rated status, you don't have the necessary 'Need to Know' qualification."

"The hell I don't! 'Need to Know' is what I've got most of."

But he wouldn't budge, so finally I said in disgust, "I don't think there is such a thing. I think you just had a belch back up on you."

He stared at me solemnly for a while, then he said, "Danny."

"Huh?"

"I'm going to tell you. Just remember your 'Alpha' status, boy. I'm going to tell you because it can't hurt anything and I want you to realize that it couldn't possibly be of use to you in your problem. It's time travel, all right, but it's not practical. You can't use it."

"Why not?"

"Give me a chance, will you? They never smoothed the bugs out of it and it's not even theoretically possible that they ever will. It's of no practical value whatsoever, even for research. It's a mere by-product of NullGrav—that's why they classified it."

"But, hell, NullGrav is declassified."

"What's that got to do with it? If this was commercial, too, maybe they'd unwrap it. But shut up."

I'm afraid I didn't, but I'd better tell this as if I had. During Chuck's senior year at the University of Colorado—Boulder, that is—he had earned extra money as a lab assistant. They had a big cryogenics lab there and at first he had worked in that. But the school had a juicy defense contract concerned with the Edinburgh field theory and they had built a big new physics laboratory in the mountains out of town. Chuck was reassigned there to Professor Twitchell—Dr. Hubert Twitchell, the man who just missed the Nobel Prize and got nasty about it.

"Twitch got the notion that if he polarized around another axis he could reverse the gravitational field instead of leveling it off. Nothing happened. So he fed what he had done back into the computer and got wild-eyed at the results. He never showed them to me, of course. He put two silver dollars into the test cage—they still used hard money around those parts then—after making me mark them. He punched the solenoid button and they disappeared.

"Now that is not much of a trick," Chuck went on. "Properly, he should have followed up by making them reappear out of the nose of a little boy who volunteers to come up on the stage. But he seemed satisfied, so I was—I was paid by the hour.

"A week later one of those cart wheels reappeared. Just one. But before that, one afternoon while I was cleaning up after he had gone home, a guinea pig showed up in the cage. It didn't belong in the lab and I hadn't seen it around before, so I took it over to the bio lab on my way home. They counted and weren't short any pigs, although it's hard to be certain with guinea pigs, so I took it home and made a pet out of it.

"After that single silver dollar came back Twitch got so worked up he quit shaving. Next time he used two guinea pigs from the bio lab. One of them looked awfully familiar to me, but I didn't see it long because he pushed the panic button and they both disappeared.

"When one of them came back about ten days later—the one that didn't look like mine—Twitch knew for sure that he had it. Then the resident O-in-C for the department of defense came around—a chair-type colonel who used to be a professor himself, of botany. Very military type . . . Twitch had no use for him. This colonel swore us both to double-dyed secrecy, over and above our 'status' oaths. He seemed to think that he had the greatest thing in military logistics since Caesar invented the carbon copy. His idea was that you could send divisions forward or back to a battle you had lost, or were going to lose, and save the day. The enemy would never figure out what had happened. He was crazy in hearts and spades, of course . . . and he didn't get the star he was bucking for. But the 'Critically Secret' classification he stuck on it stayed, so far as I know, right up to the present. I've never seen a disclosure on it."

"It might have some military use," I argued, "it seems to me, if you could engineer it to take a division of soldiers at a time. No, wait a minute, I see the hitch. You always had 'em paired. It would take two divisions, one to go forward, one to go back. One division you would lose entirely . . . I suppose it would be more practical to have a division at the right place at the right time in the first place."

"You're right, but your reasons are wrong. You don't have to use two divisions or two guinea pigs or two anything. You simply have to match the masses. You could use a division of men and a pile of rocks that weighed as much. It's an action-reaction situation, corollary with Newton's Third Law." He started drawing in the beer drippings again. "MV equals mv . . . the basic rocketship formula. The cognate time-travel formula is MT equals mt."

"I still don't see the hitch. Rocks are cheap."

"Use your head, Danny. With a rocket ship you can aim the kinkin' thing. But which direction is last week? Point to it. Just try. You haven't the slightest idea which mass is going back and which one is going forward. There's no way to orient the equipment."

I shut up. It would be embarrassing to a general to expect a division of fresh shock troops and get nothing but a pile of gravel. No wonder the ex-prof never made brigadier. But Chuck was still talking:

"You treat the two masses like the plates of a condenser, bringing them up to the same temporal potential. Then you discharge them on a damping curve that is effectively vertical. *Smacko!* —one of them heads for the middle of next year, the other one is history. But you never know which one. But that's not the worst of it; you can't come back."

"Huh? Who wants to come back?"

"Look, what use is it for research if you can't come back? Or for commerce? Either way you jump, your money is no good and you can't possibly get in touch with where you started. No equipment—and believe me it takes equipment and power. We took power from the Arco reactors. Expensive . . . that's another drawback."

"You could get back," I pointed out, "with cold sleep."

"Huh? *If* you went to the past. You might go the other way; you never know. *If* you went a short enough time back so that they had cold sleep . . . no farther back than the war. But what's the point of that? You want to know something about 1980, say, you ask somebody or you look it up in old newspapers. Now if there was some way to photograph the Crucifixion . . . but there isn't.

Not possible. Not only couldn't you get back, but there isn't that much power on the globe. There's an inverse-square law tied up in it too."

"Nevertheless, some people would try it just for the hell of it. Didn't anybody ever ride it?"

Chuck glanced around again. "I've talked too much already."

"A little more won't hurt."

"I think three people tried it. I *think*. One of them was an instructor. I was in the lab when Twitch and this bird, Leo Vincent, came in; Twitch told me I could go home. I hung around outside. After a while Twitch came out and Vincent didn't. So far as I know, he's still in there. He certainly wasn't teaching at Boulder after that."

"How about the other two?"

"Students. They all three went in together; only Twitch came out. But one of them was in class the next day, whereas the other one was missing for a week. Figure it out yourself."

"Weren't you ever tempted?"

"Me? Does my head look flat? Twitch suggested that it was almost my duty, in the interests of science, to volunteer. I said no, thanks; I'd take a short beer instead . . . but that I would gladly throw the switch for him. He didn't take me up on it."

"I'd take a chance on it. I could check up on what's worrying me . . . and then come back again by cold sleep. It would be worth it."

Chuck sighed deeply. "No more beer for you, my friend; you're drunk. You didn't listen to me. One,"—he started making tallies on the table top—"you have no way of knowing that you'd go back; you might go forward instead."

"I'd risk that. I like now a lot better than I liked then; I might like thirty years from now still better."

"Okay, so take the Long Sleep again; it's safer. Or just sit tight and wait for it to roll around; that's what I'm going to do. But quit interrupting me. Two, even if you did go back, you might miss 1970 by quite a margin. So far as I know, Twitch was shooting in the dark; I don't think he had it calibrated. But of course I was just the flunky. Three, that lab was in a stand of pine trees and it was built in 1980. Suppose you come out ten years before it was built in the middle of a western yellow pine? Ought to make quite an explosion, about like a cobalt bomb, huh? Only you wouldn't know it."

"But—— As a matter of fact, I don't see why you would come out anywhere near the lab. Why not to the spot in outer space corresponding to where the lab used to be—I mean where it was . . . or rather——"

"You don't mean anything. You stay on the world line you were on. Don't worry about the math; just remember what that guinea pig *did*. But if you go back before the lab was built, maybe you wind up in a tree. Four, how could you get back to now even with cold sleep, even if you did go the right way, arrive at the right time, and live through it?"

"Huh? I did once, why not twice?"

"Sure. But what are you going to use for money?"

I opened my mouth and closed it. That one made me feel foolish. I had had the money once; I had it no longer. Even what I had saved (not nearly enough) I could not take with me—shucks, even if I robbed a bank (an art I knew nothing about) and took a million of the best back with me, I couldn't spend it in 1970. I'd simply wind up in jail for trying to shove funny money. They had even changed the shape, not to mention serial numbers, dates, colors, and designs. "Maybe I'd just have to save it up."

"Good boy. And while you were saving it, you'd probably wind up here and now again without half trying . . . but minus your hair and your teeth."

"Okay, okay. But let's go back to that last point. Was there ever a big explosion on that spot? Where the lab was?"

"No, I don't think so."

"Then I *wouldn't* wind up in a tree—because I *didn't*. Follow me?"

"I'm three jumps ahead of you. The old time paradox again, only I won't buy it. I've thought about theory of time, too, maybe more than you have. You've got it just backward. There wasn't any explosion and you aren't going to wind up in a tree . . . because *you aren't ever going to make the jump*. Do *you* follow *me?*"

"But suppose I did?"

"You won't. Because of my fifth point. It's the killer, so listen closely. You ain't about to make any such jump because the whole thing is classified and you *can't*. They won't let you. So let's forget it, Danny. It's been a very interesting intellectual evening and the FBI will be looking for me in the morning. So let's have one more round and Monday morning if I'm still out of jail I'll phone the chief engineer over at Aladdin and find out the first name of this other 'D. B. Davis' character and who he was or is. He might even be working there and, if so, we'll have lunch with him and talk shop. I want you to meet Springer, the chief over at Aladdin, anyway; he's a good boy. And forget this time-travel nonsense; they'll never get the bugs out of it. I should never have mentioned it . . . and if you ever say I did I'll look you square in the eye and call you a liar. I might need my classified status again some-day."

So we had another beer. By the time I was home and had taken a shower and had washed some of the beer out of my system I knew he was right. Time travel was about as practical a solution to my difficulties as cutting your throat to cure a headache. More important, Chuck would find out what I wanted to know from Mr. Springer just over chops and a salad, no sweat, no expense, no risk. And I liked the year I was living in.

When I climbed into bed I reached out and got the week's stack of papers. The *Times* came to me by tube each morning, now that I was a solid citizen. I didn't read it very much, because whenever I got my head soaked full of some engineering problem, which was usually, the daily fripperies you find in the news merely annoyed me, either by boring me or, worse still, by being interesting enough to distract my mind from its proper work.

Nevertheless, I never threw out a newspaper until I had at least glanced at the headlines and checked the vital-statistics column, the latter not for births, deaths, and marriages, but simply for "withdrawals," people coming out of cold sleep. I had a notion that someday I would see the name of someone I had known back then, and then I would go around and say hello, bid him welcome, and see if I could give him a hand. The chances were against it, of course, but I kept on doing it and it always gave me a feeling of satisfaction.

I think that subconsciously I thought of all other Sleepers as my "kinfolk," the way anybody who once served in the same outfit is your buddy, at least to the extent of a drink.

There wasn't much in the papers, except the ship that was still missing between here and Mars, and that was not news but a sad lack of it. Nor did I spot any old friends among the newly awakened Sleepers. So I lay back and waited for the light to go out.

About three in the morning I sat up very suddenly, wide awake. The light came on and I blinked at it. I had had a very odd dream, not quite a nightmare but nearly, of having failed to notice little Ricky in the vital statistics.

I knew I hadn't. But just the same when I looked over and saw the week's stack of newspapers still sitting there I was greatly relieved; it had been possible that I had stuffed them down the chute before going to sleep, as I sometimes did.

I dragged them back onto the bed and started reading the vital statistics again. This time I read all categories, births, deaths, marriages, divorces, adoptions, changes of name, commitments, and withdrawals, for it had occurred to me that my eye might have caught Ricky's name without consciously realizing it, while glancing down the column to the only subhead I was interested in— Ricky might have got married or had a baby or something.

I almost missed what must have caused the distressing dream. It was in the *Times* for 2 May, 2001, Tuesday's withdrawals listed in Wednesday's paper: "Riverside Sanctuary . . . F. V. Heinicke."

"*F. V. Heinicke!*"

"Heinicke" was Ricky's grandmother's name . . . I knew it, I was *certain* of it! I didn't know *why* I knew it. But I felt that it had been buried in my head and had not popped up until I read it again. I had probably seen it or heard it at some time from Ricky or Miles, or it was even possible that I had met the old gal at Sandia. No matter, the name, seen in the *Times,* had fitted a forgotten piece of information in my brain and then I *knew.*

Only I still had to prove it. I had to make sure that "F. V. Heinicke" stood for "Frederica Virginia Heinicke."

I was shaking with excitement, anticipation, and fear. In spite of well-established new habits I tried to zip my clothes instead of sticking the seams together and made a botch of getting dressed. But a few minutes later I was down in the hall where the phone booth was—I didn't have an instrument in my room or I would have used it; I was simply a supplementary listing for the house phone. Then I had to run back up again when I found that I had forgotten my phone-credit ID card—I was really disorganized.

Then, when I had it, I was trembling so that I could hardly fit it into the slot. But I did and signaled "Service."

"Circuit desired?"

"Uh, I want the Riverside Sanctuary. That's in Riverside Borough."

"Searching . . . holding . . . circuit free. We are signaling."

The screen lighted up at last and a man looked grumpily at me. "You must have the wrong phasing. This is the sanctuary. We're closed for the night."

I said, "Hang on, *please*. If this is the Riverside Sanctuary, you're just who I want."

"Well, what do you want? At this hour?"

"You have a client there, F. V. Heinicke, a new withdrawal. I want to know——"

He shook his head. "We don't give out information about clients over the phone. And certainly not in the middle of the night. You'd better call after ten o'clock. Better yet, come here."

"I will, I will. But I want to know just one thing. What do the initials "F. V." stand for?"

"I told you that——"

"Will you *listen*, please? I'm not just butting in; I'm a Sleeper myself. Sawtelle. Withdrawn just lately. So I know all about the 'confidential relationship' and what's proper. Now you've already published this client's name in the paper. You and I both know that the sanctuaries always give the papers the full names of clients withdrawn and committed . . . but the papers trim the given names to initials to save space. Isn't that true?"

He thought about it. "Could be."

"Then what possible harm is there in telling me what the initials "F. V." stand for?"

He hesitated still longer. "None, I guess, if that's all you want. It's all you're going to get. Hold on."

He passed out of the screen, was gone for what seemed like an hour, came back holding a card. "The light's poor," he said, peering at it. " 'Frances'—no, 'Frederica.' 'Frederica Virginia.' "

My ears roared and I almost fainted. "Thank God!"

"You all right?"

"Yes. Thank you. Thank you from the bottom of my heart. Yes, I'm all right."

"Hmm. I guess there's no harm in telling you one more thing. It might save you a trip. She's already checked out."

IX

I could have saved time by hiring a cab to jump me to Riverside, but I was handicapped by lack of cash. I was living in West Hollywood; the nearest twenty-four-hour bank was downtown at the Grand Circle of the Ways. So first I rode the Ways downtown and went to the bank for cash. One real improvement I had not appreciated up to then was the universal checkbook system; with a single cybernet as clearinghouse for the whole city and radio-active coding on my checkbook, I got cash laid in my palm as quickly there as I could have gotten it at my home bank across from Hired Girl, Inc.

Then I caught the express Way for Riverside. When I reached the sanctuary it was just daylight.

There was nobody there but the night technician I had talked to and his wife, the night nurse. I'm afraid I didn't make a good impression. I had a day's beard, I was wild-eyed, I probably had a beer breath, and I had not worked out a consistent framework of lies.

Nevertheless, Mrs. Larrigan, the night nurse, was sympathetic and helpful. She got a photograph out of file and said, "Is this your cousin, Mr. Davis?"

It was Ricky. There was no doubt about it, it was Ricky! Oh, not the Ricky I had known, for this was not a little girl but a mature young woman, twentyish or older, with a grown-up hairdo and a grown-up and very beautiful face. She was smiling.

But her eyes were unchanged and the ageless pixie quality of her face that had made her so delightful a child was still there. It was the same face, matured, filled out, grown beautiful, but unmistakable.

The stereo blurred, my eyes had filled with tears. "Yes," I managed to choke. "Yes. That's Ricky."

Mr. Larrigan said, "Nancy, you shouldn't have showed him that."

"Pooh, Hank, what harm is there in showing a photograph?"

"You know the rules." He turned to me. "Mister, as I told you on the phone, we don't give out information about clients. You come back here at ten o'clock when the administration office opens."

"Or you could come back at eight," his wife added. "Dr. Bernstein will be here then."

"Now, Nancy, you just keep quiet. If he wants information, the man to see is the director. Bernstein hasn't any more business answering questions than we have. Besides, she wasn't even Bernstein's patient."

"Hank, you're being fussy. You men like rules just for the sake of rules. If he's in a hurry to see her, he could be in Brawley by ten o'clock." She turned to me. "You come back at eight. That's best. My husband and I can't really tell you anything anyhow."

"What's this about Brawley? Did she go to Brawley?"

If her husband had not been there I think she would have told me more. She hesitated and he looked stern. She answered, "You see Dr. Bernstein. If you haven't had breakfast, there's a real nice place just down the street."

So I went to the "real nice place" (it was) and ate and used their washroom and bought a tube of *Beardgo* from a dispenser in the washroom and a shirt from another dispenser and threw away the one I had been wearing. By the time I returned I was fairly respectable.

But Larrigan must have bent Dr. Bernstein's ear about me. He was a young man, resident in training, and he took a very stiff line. "Mr. Davis, you claim to be a Sleeper yourself. You must certainly know that there are criminals who make a regular business of preying on the gullibility and lack of orientation of a newly awakened Sleeper. Most Sleepers have considerable assets, all of them are unworldly in the world in which they find themselves, they are usually lonely and a bit scared—a perfect setup for confidence men."

"But all I want to know is where she went! I'm her cousin. But I took the Sleep before she did, so I didn't know she was going to."

"They usually claim to be relatives." He looked at me closely. "Haven't I seen you before?"

"I strongly doubt it. Unless you just happened to pass me on the Ways, downtown." People are always thinking they've seen me before; I've got one of the Twelve Standard Faces, as lacking in uniqueness as one peanut in a sackful. "Doctor, how about phoning Dr. Albrecht at Sawtelle Sanctuary and checking on me?"

He looked judicial. "You come back and see the director. He can call the Sawtelle Sanctuary . . . or the police, whichever he sees fit."

So I left. Then I may have made a mistake. Instead of coming back to see the director and very possibly getting the exact information I needed (with the aid of Albrecht's vouching for me), I hired a jumpcab and went straight to Brawley.

It took three days to pick up her trail in Brawley. Oh, she had lived there and so had her grandmother; I found that out quickly. But the grandmother had died twenty years earlier and Ricky had taken the Sleep. Brawley is a mere hundred thousand compared with the seven million of Great Los Angeles; the twenty-year-old records were not hard to find. It was the trail less than a week old that I had trouble with.

Part of the trouble was that she was with someone; I had been looking for a young woman traveling alone. When I found out she had a man with her I thought anxiously about the crooks preying on Sleepers that Bernstein had lectured me about and got busier than ever.

I followed a false lead to Calexico, went back to Brawley, started over, picked it up again, and traced them as far as Yuma.

At Yuma I gave up the chase, for Ricky had gotten married. What I saw on the register at the county clerk's office there shocked me so much that I dropped everything and jumped a ship for Denver, stopping only to mail a card to Chuck telling him to clear out my desk and pack the stuff in my room.

I stopped in Denver just long enough to visit a dental-supply house. I had not been in Denver since it had become the capital —after the Six Weeks War, Miles and I had gone straight to California—and the place stunned me. Why, I couldn't even find Colfax Avenue. I had understood that everything essential to the government was buried back under the Rockies. If that is so, then there must be an awful lot of nonessentials still aboveground; the place seemed even more crowded than Great Los Angeles.

At the dental-supply house I bought ten kilograms of gold, isotope 197, in the form of fourteen-gauge wire. I paid $86.10 a kilogram for it, which was decidedly too much, since gold of engineering quality was selling for around $70 a kilogram, and the transaction mortally wounded my only thousand-dollar bill. But engineering gold comes either in alloys never found in nature, or with isotopes 196 and 198 present, or both, depending on the application. For my purposes I wanted fine gold, undetectable from gold refined from natural ore, and I did not want gold that might burn my pants off if I got cozy with it—the overdose at Sandia had given me a healthy respect for radiation poisoning.

I wound the gold wire around my waist and went to Boulder. Ten kilograms is about the weight of a well-filled weekend bag and that much gold bulks almost exactly the same as a quart of milk. But the wire form of it made it bulk more than it would have solid; I can't recommend it as a girdle. But gold slugs would have been still harder to carry, and this way it was always with me.

Dr. Twitchell was still living there, though no longer working; he was professor emeritus and spent most of his waking hours in the bar of the faculty club. It took me four days to catch him in another bar, since the faculty club was closed to outlanders like me. But when I did, it turned out to be easy to buy him a drink.

He was a tragic figure in the classic Greek meaning, a great man—a *very* great man—gone to ruin. He should have been up there with Einstein and Bohr and Newton; as it was, only a few specialists in field theory were really aware of the stature of his work. Now when I met him his brilliant mind was soured with disappointment, dimmed with age, and soggy with alcohol. It was like visiting the ruins of what had been a magnificent temple after the roof has fallen in, half the columns knocked down, and vines have grown over it all.

Nevertheless, he was brainier on the skids than I ever was at my best. I'm smart enough myself to appreciate real genius when I meet it.

The first time I saw him he looked up, looked straight at me and said, "You again."

"Sir?"

"You used to be one of my students, didn't you?"

"Why, no, sir, I never had that honor." Ordinarily when people think they have seen me before, I brush it off; this time I decided to exploit it if I could. "Perhaps you are thinking of my cousin, Doctor—class of '86. He studied under you at one time."

"Possibly. What did he major in?"

"He had to drop out without a degree, sir. But he was a great admirer of yours. He never missed a chance to tell people he had studied under you."

You can't make an enemy by telling a mother her child is beautiful. Dr. Twitchell let me sit down and presently let me buy him a drink. The greatest weakness of the glorious old wreck was his professional vanity. I had salvaged part of the four days before I could scrape up an acquaintance with him by memorizing everything there was about him in the university library, so I knew what papers he had written, where he had presented them, what earned and honorary degrees he held, and what books he had written. I had tried one of the latter, but I was already out of my depth on page nine, although I did pick up a little patter from it.

I let him know that I was a camp follower of science myself; right at present I was researching for a book: *Unsung Geniuses*.

"What's it going to be about?"

I admitted diffidently that I thought it would be appropriate to start the book with a popular account of his life and works . . . provided he would be willing to relax a bit from his well-known habit of shunning publicity. I would have to get a lot of my material from him, of course.

He thought it was claptrap and could not think of such a thing. But I pointed out that he had a duty to posterity and he agreed to think it over. By the next day he simply assumed that I was going to write his biography—not just a chapter, a whole book. From then on he talked and talked and talked and I took notes . . . real notes; I did not dare try to fool him by faking, as he sometimes asked me to read back.

But he never mentioned time travel.

Finally I said, "Doctor, isn't it true that if it had not been for a certain colonel who was once stationed here you would have had the Nobel Prize hands down?"

He cursed steadily for three minutes with magnificent style. "Who told you about him?"

"Uh, Doctor, when I was doing research writing for the Department of Defense—— I've mentioned that, haven't I?"

"No."

"Well, when I was, I heard the whole story from a young Ph.D. working in another section. He had read the report and he said it was perfectly clear that you would be the most famous name in physics today . . . if you had been permitted to publish your work."

"Hrrmph! That much is true."

"But I gathered that it was classified . . . by order of this Colonel, uh, Plushbottom."

"Thrushbotham. Thrushbotham, sir. A fat, fatuous, flatulent, foot-kissing fool incompetent to find his hat with it nailed to his head. Which it should have been."

"It seems a great pity."

"What is a pity, sir? That Thrushbotham was a fool? That was nature's doing, not mine."

"It seems a pity that the world should be deprived of the story. I understand that you are not allowed to speak of it."

"Who told you that? I say what I please!"

"That was what I understood, sir . . . from my friend in the Department of Defense."

"Hrrrmph!"

That was all I got out of him that night. It took him a week to decide to show me his laboratory.

Most of the building was now used by other researchers, but his time laboratory he had never surrendered, even though he did not use it now; he fell back on its classified status and refused to let anyone else touch it, nor had he permitted the apparatus to be torn down. When he let me in, the place smelled like a vault that has not been opened in years.

He had had just enough drinks not to give a damn, not so many but what he was still steady. His capacity was pretty high. He lectured me on the mathematics of time theory and temporal displacement (he didn't call it "time travel"), but he cautioned me not to take notes. It would not have helped if I had, as he would start a paragraph with, "It is therefore obvious——" and go on from there to matters which may have been obvious to him and God but to no one else.

When he slowed down I said, "I gathered from my friend that the one thing you had not been able to do was to calibrate it? That you could not tell the exact magnitude of the temporal displacement?"

"What? Poppycock! Young man, if you can't measure it, it's not science." He bubbled for a bit, like a teakettle, then went on, "Here. I'll *show* you." He turned away and started making adjustments. All that showed of his equipment was what he called the "temporal locus stage"—just a low platform with a cage around it—and a control board which might have served for a steam plant or a low-pressure chamber. I'm fairly sure I could have studied out how to handle the controls had I been left alone to examine them, but I had been told sharply to stay away from them. I could see an eight-point Brown recorder, some extremely heavy-duty solenoid-actuated switches, and a dozen other equally familiar components, but it didn't mean a thing without the circuit diagrams.

He turned back to me and demanded, "Have you any change in your pocket?"

I reached in and hauled out a handful. He glanced at it and selected two five-dollar pieces, mint new, the pretty green plastic hexagonals issued just that year. I could have wished that he had picked half fives, as I was running low.

"Do you have a knife?"

"Yes, sir."

"Scratch your initials on each of them."

I did so. He then had me place them side by side on the stage. "Note the exact time. I have set the displacement for exactly one week, plus or minus six seconds."

I looked at my watch. Dr. Twitchell said, "Five . . . four . . . three . . . two . . . one . . . *now!*"

I looked up from my watch. The coins were gone. I didn't have to pretend that my eyes bugged out. Chuck had told me about a similar demonstration—but seeing it was another matter.

Dr. Twitchell said briskly, "We will return here one week from tonight and wait for one of them to reappear. As for the other one—you saw both of them on the stage? You placed them there yourself?"

"Yes, sir."

"Where was I?"

"At the control board, sir." He had been a good fifteen feet from the nearest part of the cage around the stage and had not approached it since.

"Very well. Come here." I did so and he reached into a pocket. "Here's one of your bits. You'll get the other back a week from now." He handed me a green five-dollar coin; it had my initials on it.

I did not say anything because I can't talk very well with my jaw sagging loosely. He went on, "Your remarks last week disturbed me. So I visited this place on Wednesday, something I have not done for—oh, more than a year. I found this coin on the stage, so I knew that I had been . . . *would be* . . . using the equipment again. It took me until tonight to decide to demonstrate it to you."

I looked at the coin and felt it. "This was in your pocket when we came here tonight?"

"Certainly."

"But how could it be both in your pocket and my pocket at the same time?"

"Good Lord, man, have you no eyes to see with? No brain to reason with? Can't you absorb a simple fact simply because it lies outside your dull existence? You fetched it here in your pocket tonight—and we kicked into last week. You saw. A few days ago I found it here. I placed it in my pocket. I fetched it here tonight. The same coin . . . or, to be precise, a later segment of its spacetime structure, a week more worn, a week more dulled—but what the canaille would call the 'same' coin. Although no more identical in fact than is a baby identical with the man the baby grows into. Older."

144

I looked at it. "Doctor . . . push me back in time by a week."

He stared angrily. "Out of the question!"

"Why not? Won't it work with people?"

"Eh? Certainly it will work with people."

"Then why not do it? I'm not afraid. And think what a wonderful thing it would be for the book . . . if I could testify *of my own knowledge* that the Twitchell time displacement works."

"You *can* report it of your own knowledge. You just saw it."

"Yes," I admitted slowly, "but I won't be believed. That business with the coins . . . I saw it and I believe it. But anyone simply reading an account of it would conclude that I was gullible, that you had hoaxed me with some simple legerdemain."

"Damn it, sir!"

"That's what *they* would say. They wouldn't be able to believe that I actually had seen what I reported. But if you were to ship me back just a week, then I could report of my own knowledge——"

"Sit down. Listen to me." He sat down, but there was no place for me to sit, although he did not seem aware of it. "I *have* experimented with human beings long ago. And for that reason I resolved never to do it again."

"Why? Did it kill them?"

"What? Don't talk nonsense." He looked at me sharply, added, "You are not to put this in the book."

"As you say, sir."

"Some minor experiments showed that living subjects could make temporal displacements without harm. I had confided in a colleague, a young fellow who taught drawing and other matters in the school of architecture. Really more of an engineer than a scientist, but I liked him; his mind was alive. This young chap— it can't hurt to tell you his name: Leonard Vincent—was wild to try it . . . really try it; he wanted to undergo major displacement, five hundred years. I was weak. I let him."

"Then what happened?"

"How should I know? Five hundred years, man! I'll never live to find out."

"But you think he's five hundred years in the future?"

"Or the past. He might have wound up in the fifteenth century. Or the twenty-fifth. The chances are precisely even. There's an indeterminacy—symmetrical equations. I've sometimes thought . . . no, just a chance similarity in names."

I didn't ask what he meant by this because I suddenly saw the similarity, too, and my hair stood on end. Then I pushed it out of my mind; I had other problems. Besides, a chance similarity was all it could be—a man could not get from Colorado to Italy, not in the fifteenth century.

"But I resolved not to be tempted again. It wasn't science, it added nothing to the data. If he was displaced forward, well and good. But if he was displaced backward . . . then possibly I sent my friend to be killed by savages. Or eaten by wild animals."

Or even possibly, I thought, to become a "Great White God." I kept the thought to myself. "But you needn't use so long a displacement with me."

"Let's say no more about it, if you please, sir."

"As you wish, Doctor." But I couldn't drop it. "Uh, may I make a suggestion?"

"Eh? Speak up."

"We could get almost the same result by a rehearsal."

"What do you mean?"

"A complete dry run, with everything done just exactly as if you were intending to displace a living subject—I'll act out that part. We'll do everything precisely as if you meant to displace me, right up to the point where you would push that button. Then I'll understand the procedure . . . which I don't quite, as yet."

He grumbled a little but he really wanted to show off his toy. He weighed me and set aside metal weights just equal to my hundred and seventy pounds. "These are the same scales I used with poor Vincent."

Between us we placed them on one side of the stage. "What temporal setting shall we make?" he asked. "This is your show."

"Uh, you said that it could be set accurately?"

"I said so, sir. Do you doubt it?"

"Oh no, no! Well, let's see, this is the twenty-fourth of May—suppose we . . . how about, uh, say thirty-one years, three weeks, one day, seven hours, thirteen minutes, and twenty-five seconds?"

"A poor jest, sir. When I said 'accurate' I meant 'accurate to better than one part in one hundred thousand.' I have had no opportunity to calibrate to one part in nine hundred million."

"Oh. You see, Doctor, how important an exact rehearsal is to me, since I know so little about it. Uh, suppose we call it thirty-one years and three weeks. Or is that still too finicky?"

"Not at all. The maximum error should not exceed two hours." He made his adjustments. "You can take your place on the stage."

"Is that all?"

"Yes. All but the power. I could not actually make this displacement with the line voltage I used on those coins. But since we aren't actually going to do it, that doesn't matter."

I looked disappointed and was. "Then you don't actually have what is necessary to produce such a displacement? You were speaking theoretically?"

"Confound it, sir, I was not speaking theoretically."

"But if you don't have the power . . . ?"

"I can get the power if you insist. Wait." He went to a corner of the lab and picked up a phone. It must have been installed when the lab was new; I hadn't seen one like it since I was awakened. There followed a brisk conversation with the night superintendent of the university's powerhouse. Dr. Twitchell was not dependent on profanity; he could avoid it entirely and be more biting than most real artists can be when using plainer words. "I am not in the least interested in your opinions, my man. Read your instructions. I have full facilities whenever I wish them. Or can you read? Shall we meet with the president at ten tomorrow morning and have him read them to you? Oh? So you *can* read? Can you write as well? Or have we exhausted your talents? Then write this down: Emergency full power across the bus bars of the Thornton Memorial Laboratory in exactly eight minutes. Repeat that back."

He replaced the instrument. "People!"

He went to the control board, made some changes, and waited. Presently, even from where I stood inside the cage, I could see the long hands of three sets of meters swing across their dials and a red light came on at the top of the board. "Power," he announced.

"Now what happens?"

"Nothing."

"That's just what I thought."

"What do you mean?"

"What I said. Nothing would happen."

"I'm afraid I don't understand you. I hope I don't understand you. What I meant is that nothing would happen unless I closed this pilot switch. If I did, you would be displaced precisely thirty-one years, three weeks."

"And I still say nothing would happen."

His face grew dark. "I think, sir, you are being intentionally offensive."

"Call it what you want to. Doctor, I came here to investigate a remarkable rumor. Well, I've investigated it. I've seen a control board with pretty lights on it; it looks like a set for a mad scientist in a grabbie spectacular. I've seen a parlor trick performed with a couple of coins. Not much of a trick, by the way, since you selected the coins yourself and told me how to mark them; any parlor magician could do better. I've heard a lot of talk. But talk is cheap. What you claim to have discovered is impossible. By the way, they know that down at the department. Your report wasn't suppressed; it's simply filed in the screwball file. They get it out and pass it around now and then for a laugh."

I thought the poor old boy was going to have a stroke there and then. But I had to stimulate him by the only reflex he had left, his vanity.

"Come out of there, sir. Come out. I'm going to thrash you. With my bare hands I'm going to thrash you."

The rage he was in, I think he might have managed it, despite age and weight and physical condition. But I answered, "You don't scare me, Pappy. That dummy button doesn't scare me either. Go ahead and push it."

He looked at me, looked at the button, but still he didn't do anything. I snickered and said, "A hoax, just as the boys said it was. Twitch, you're a pompous old faker, a stuffed shirt. Colonel Thrushbotham was right."

That did it.

X

Even as he stabbed at the button I tried to shout at him not to do it. But it was too late; I was already falling. My last thought was an agonized one that I didn't want to go through with it. I had chucked away everything and tormented almost to death a poor old man who hadn't done me any harm—and I didn't even know which way I was going. Worse, I didn't know that I would get there.

Then I hit. I don't think I fell more than four feet but I had not been ready for it. I fell like a stick, collapsed like a sack.

Then somebody was saying, "Where the devil did *you* come from?"

It was a man, about forty, bald-headed but well built and lean. He was standing facing me with his fists on his hipbones. He looked competent and shrewd and his face was not unpleasant save that at the moment he seemed sore at me.

I sat up and found that I was sitting on granite gravel and pine needles. There was a woman standing by the man, a pleasant pretty woman somewhat younger than he. She was looking at me wide-eyed but not speaking.

"Where am I?" I said foolishly. I could have said, "When am I?" but that would have sounded still more foolish, and besides, I didn't think of it. One look at them and I knew when I was *not*—

I was sure it was not 1970. Nor was I still in 2001; in 2001 they kept that sort of thing for the beaches. So I must have gone the wrong way.

Because neither one of them wore anything but smooth coats of tan. Not even Sticktite. But they seemed to find it enough. Certainly they were not embarrassed by it.

"One thing at a time," he objected. "I asked you how you got here?" He glanced up. "Your parachute didn't stick in the trees, did it? In any case, what are you doing here? This is posted private property; you're trespassing. And what are you doing in that Mardi Gras getup?"

I didn't see anything wrong with my clothes—especially in view of the way they were dressed. But I didn't answer. Other times, other customs—I could see that I was going to have trouble.

She put a hand on his arm. "Don't, John," she said gently. "I think he's hurt."

He looked at her, glanced back sharply at me. "Are you hurt?"

I tried to stand up, managed it. "I don't think so. A few bruises, maybe. Uh, what date is today?"

"Huh? Why, it's the first Sunday in May. The third of May, I think. Is that right, Jenny?"

"Yes, dear."

"Look," I said urgently, "I got an awful knock on the head. I'm confused. What's the date? The whole date?"

"What?"

I should have kept my mouth shut until I could pick it up off something, a calendar or a paper. But I had to know right then; I couldn't stand to wait. "What year?"

"Brother, you did get a lump. It's 1970." I saw him staring at my clothes again.

My relief was almost more than I could stand. I'd made it, I'd made it! I wasn't too late. "Thanks," I said. "Thanks an awful lot. You don't know." He still looked as if he wanted to call out the reserves, so I added nervously, "I'm subject to sudden attacks of amnesia. Once I lost, uh—five whole years."

"I should think that would be upsetting," he said slowly. "Do you feel well enough to answer my questions?"

"Don't badger him, dear," she said softly. "He looks like a nice person. I think he's just made a mistake."

"We'll see. Well?"

"I feel all right . . . now. But I was pretty confused for a minute there."

"Okay. How did you get here? And why are you dressed that way?"

"To tell the truth, I'm not sure how I got here. And I certainly don't know where I am. These spells hit me suddenly. As for how I'm dressed . . . I guess you could call it personal eccentricity. Uh . . . like the way you're dressed. Or not dressed."

He glanced down at himself and grinned. "Oh, yes. I'm quite aware that the way my wife and I are dressed . . . or not dressed . . . would call for explanation under some circumstances. But we prefer to make trespassers do the explaining instead. You see, you don't belong here, dressed that way or any other, while we do—just as we are. These are the grounds of the Denver Sunshine Club."

John and Jenny Sutton were the sort of sophisticated, unshockable, friendly people who could invite an earthquake in for tea. John obviously was not satisfied with my fishy explanations and wanted to cross-examine me, but Jenny held him back. I stuck to my story about "dizzy spells" and said that the last I remembered was yesterday evening and that I had been in Denver, at the New Brown Palace. Finally he said, "Well, it's quite interesting, even exciting, and I suppose somebody who's going into Boulder can drop you there and you can get a bus back into Denver." He looked at me again. "But if I take you back to the clubhouse, people are going to be mighty, mighty curious."

I looked down at myself. I had been made vaguely uneasy by the fact that I was dressed and they were not—I mean I felt like the one out of order, not they. "John . . . would it simplify things if I peeled off my clothes too?" The prospect did not upset me; I had never been in one of the bare-skin camps before, seeing no point in them. But Chuck and I had spent a couple of weekends at Santa Barbara and one at Laguna Beach—at a beach skin makes sense and nothing else does.

He nodded. "It certainly would."

"Dear," said Jenny, "he could be our guest."

"Mmm . . . yes. My only love, you paddle your sweet self into the grounds. Mix around and manage to let it be known that we are expecting a guest from . . . where had it better be, Danny?"

"Uh, from California. Los Angeles. I actually am from there." I almost said "Great Los Angeles" and realized that I was going to have to guard my speech. "Movies" were no longer "grabbies."

"From Los Angeles. That and 'Danny' is all that is necessary; we don't use last names, unless offered. So, honey, you spread the word, as if it were something everybody already knew. Then in about half an hour you have to meet us down by the gate. But come here instead. And fetch my overnight bag."

"Why the bag, dear?"

"To conceal that masquerade costume. It's pretty conspicuous, even for anyone who is as eccentric as Danny said he is."

I got up and went at once behind some bushes to undress, since I wouldn't have any excuse for locker-room modesty once Jenny Sutton left us. I had to do it; I couldn't peel down and reveal that I had twenty thousand dollars' worth of gold, figured at the 1970 standard of sixty dollars an ounce, wrapped around my waist. It did not take long, as I had made a belt out of the gold, instead of a girdle, the first time I had had trouble getting it off and on to bathe; I had double-looped it and wired it together in front.

When I had my clothes off I wrapped the gold in them and tried to pretend that it all weighed only what clothes should. John Sutton glanced at the bundle but said nothing. He offered me a cigarette—he carried them strapped to his ankle. They were a brand I had never expected to see again.

I waved it but it didn't light. Then I let him light it for me. "Now," he said quietly, "that we are alone, do you have anything you want to tell me? If I'm going to vouch for you to the club, I'm honor-bound to be sure, at the very least, that you won't make trouble."

I took a puff. It felt raw in my throat. "John, I won't make any trouble. That's the last thing on earth that I want."

"Mmm . . . probably. Just 'dizzy spells' then?"

I thought about it. It was an impossible situation. The man had a right to know. But he certainly would not believe the truth . . . at least I would not have in his shoes. But it would be worse if he *did* believe me; it would kick up the very hoorah that I did not want. I suppose that if I had been a real, honest, legitimate time traveler, engaged in scientific research, I would have sought publicity, brought along indisputable proof, and invited tests by scientists.

But I wasn't; I was a private and somewhat shady citizen, engaged in hanky-panky I didn't want to call attention to. I was simply looking for my Door into Summer, as quietly as possible.

"John, you wouldn't believe it if I told you."

"Mmm . . . perhaps. Still, I saw a man fall out of empty sky . . . but he didn't hit hard enough to hurt him. He's wearing funny clothes. He doesn't seem to know where he is or what day it is. Danny, I've read Charles Fort, the same as most people. But I never expected to meet a case. But, having met one, I don't expect the explanation to be as simple as a card trick. So?"

"John, something you said earlier—the way you phrased something—made me think you were a lawyer."

"Yes, I am. Why?"

"Can I make a privileged communication?"

"Hmm—are you asking me to accept you as a client?"

"If you want to put it that way, yes. I'm probably going to need advice."

"Shoot. Privileged."

"Okay. I'm from the future. Time travel."

He didn't say anything for several moments. We were lying stretched out in the sun. I was doing it to keep warm; May in Colorado is sunshiny but brisk. John Sutton seemed used to it and was simply lounging, chewing a pine needle.

"You're right," he answered. "I don't believe it. Let's stick to 'dizzy spells.'"

"I told you you wouldn't."

He sighed. "Let's say I don't want to. I don't want to believe in ghosts, either, or reincarnation, or any of this ESP magic. I like simple things that I can understand. I think most people do. So my first advice to you is to keep it a privileged communication. Don't spread it around."

"That suits me."

He rolled over. "But I think it would be a good idea if we burned these clothes. I'll find you something to wear. Will they burn?"

"Uh, not very easily. They'll melt."

"Better put your shoes back on. We wear shoes mostly, and those will get by. Anybody asks you questions about them, they're custom-made. Health shoes."

"They are, both."

"Okay." He started to unroll my clothes before I could stop him. "What the devil!"

It was too late, so I let him uncover it. "Danny," he said in a queer voice, "is this stuff what it appears to be?"

"What does it appear to be?"

"Gold."

"Yes."

"Where did you get it?"

"I bought it."

He felt it, tried the dead softness of the stuff, sensuous as putty, then hefted it. "Cripes! Danny . . . listen to me carefully. I'm going to ask you one question, and be damned careful how you answer it. Because I've got no use for a client who lies to me. I dump him. And I won't be a party to a felony. Did you come by this stuff legally?"

"Yes."

"Maybe you haven't heard of the Gold Reserve Act of 1968?"

"I have. I came by it legally. I intend to sell it to the Denver Mint, for dollars."

"Jeweler's license, maybe?"

"No. John, I told the simple truth, whether you believe me or not. Where I came from I bought that over the counter, legal as breathing. Now I want to turn it in for dollars at the earliest possible moment. I know that it is against the law to keep it. What can they do to me if I lay it on the counter at the mint and tell them to weigh it?"

"Nothing, in the long run . . . if you stick to your 'dizzy spells.' But they can surely make your life miserable in the meantime." He looked at it. "I think you had better kick a little dirt over it."

"Bury it?"

"You don't have to go that far. But if what you tell me is true, you found this stuff in the mountains. That's where prospectors usually find gold."

"Well . . . whatever you say. I don't mind some little white lies, since it is legitimately mine anyhow."

"But is it a lie? When did you first lay eyes on this gold? What was the earliest date when it was in your possession?"

I tried to think back. It was the same day I left Yuma, which was sometime in May, 2001. About two weeks ago. . . .

Hunh!

"Put that way, John . . . the earliest date on which I saw that gold . . . was today, May third, 1970."

He nodded. "So you found it in the mountains."

The Suttons were staying over until Monday morning, so I stayed over. The other club members were all friendly but remarkably unnosy about my personal affairs, less so than any group I've ever been in. I've learned since that this constitutes standard good manners in a skin club, but at the time it made them the most discreet and most polite people I had ever met.

John and Jenny had their own cabin and I slept on a cot in the clubhouse dormitory. It was darn chilly. The next morning John gave me a shirt and a pair of blue jeans. My own clothes were wrapped around the gold in a bag in the trunk of his car—which itself was a Jaguar Imperator, all I needed to tell me that he was no cheap shyster. But I had known that by his manner.

I stayed overnight with them and by Tuesday I had a little money. I never laid eyes on the gold again, but in the course of the next few weeks John turned over to me its exact mint value as bullion minus the standard fees of licensed gold buyers. I know that he did not deal with the mint directly, as he always turned over to me vouchers from gold buyers. He did not deduct for his own services and he never offered to tell me the details.

I did not care. Once I had cash again, I got busy. That first Tuesday, 5 May, 1970, Jenny drove me around and I rented a small loft in the old commercial district. I equipped it with a drafting table, a workbench, an army cot, and darn little else; it already had 120, 240, gas, running water, and a toilet that stopped up easily. I didn't want any more and I had to watch every dime.

It was tedious and time-wasting to design by the old compass-and-T-square routine and I didn't have a minute to spare, so I built *Drafting Dan* before I rebuilt *Flexible Frank*. Only this time *Flexible Frank* became *Protean Pete*, the all-purpose automaton, so linked as to be able to do almost anything a man can do, provided its Thorsen tubes were properly instructed. I knew that *Protean Pete* would not stay that way; his descendants would evolve into a horde of specialized gadgets, but I wanted to make the claims as broad as possible.

Working models are not required for patents, merely drawings and descriptions. But I needed good models, models that would work perfectly and anybody could demonstrate, because these models were going to have to sell themselves, show by their very practicality and by the evident economy designed into them for their eventual production engineering that they would not only work but would be a good investment—the patent office is stuffed with things that work but are worthless commercially.

The work went both fast and slow, fast because I knew exactly what I was doing, slow because I did not have a proper machine shop nor any help. Presently I grudgingly dipped into my precious cash to rent some machine tools, then things went better. I worked from breakfast to exhaustion, seven days a week, except for about one weekend a month with John and Jenny at the bare-bottom club near Boulder. By the first of September I had both models working properly and was ready to start on the drawings and descriptions. I designed and sent out for manufacture pretty speckle-lacquer cover plates for both of them and I had the external moving parts chrome-plated; these were the only jobs I farmed out and it hurt me to spend the money, but I felt that it was necessary. Oh, I had made extreme use of catalogue-available standard components; I could not have built them otherwise, nor would they have been commercial when I got through. But I did not like to spend money on custom-made prettiness.

I did not have time to get around much, which was just as well. Once when I was out buying a servo motor I ran into a chap I had known in California. He spoke to me and I answered before I thought. "Hey, Dan! Danny Davis! Imagine bumping into you here. I thought you were in Mojave?"

I shook hands. "Just a quick business trip. I'm going back in a few days."

"I'm going back this afternoon. I'll phone Miles and tell him I saw you."

I looked worried and was. "Don't do that, please."

"Why not? Aren't you and Miles still buddy-buddy budding tycoons together?"

"Well . . . look, Mort, Miles doesn't know I'm here. I'm supposed to be in Albuquerque on business for the company. But I flew up here on the side, on strictly personal and private business. Get me? Nothing to do with the firm. And I don't care to discuss it with Miles."

He looked knowing. "Woman trouble?"

"Well . . . yes."

"She married?"

"You might say so."

He dug me in the ribs and winked. "I catch. Old Miles is pretty puritanical, isn't he? Okay, I'll cover for you and someday you can cover for me. Is she any good?"

I'd like to cover you with a spade, I thought to myself, you fourth-rate frallup. Mort was the sort of no-good traveling salesman who spends more time trying to seduce waitresses than taking care of his customers—besides which, the line he handled was as shoddy as he was, never up to its specs.

But I bought him a drink and treated him to fairy tales about the "married woman" I had invented and listened while he boasted to me of no doubt equally fictitious exploits. Then I shook him.

On another occasion I tried to buy Dr. Twitchell a drink and failed.

I had seated myself beside him at the restaurant counter of a drugstore on Champa Street, then caught sight of his face in the mirror. My first impulse was to crawl under the counter and hide.

Then I caught hold of myself and realized that, out of all the persons living in 1970, he was the one I had least need to worry about. Nothing could go wrong because nothing had . . . I meant "nothing would." No—— Then I quit trying to phrase it, realizing that if time travel ever became widespread, English grammar was going to have to add a whole new set of tenses to describe reflexive situations—conjugations that would make the French literary tenses and the Latin historical tenses look simple.

In any case, past or future or something else, Twitchell was not a worry to me now. I could relax.

I studied his face in the mirror, wondering if I had been misled by a chance resemblance. But I had not been. Twitchell did not have a general-issue face like mine; he had stern, self-assured, slightly arrogant and quite handsome features which would have looked at home on Zeus. I remembered that face only in ruins, but there was no doubt—and I squirmed inside as I thought of the old man and how badly I had treated him. I wondered how I could make it up to him.

Twitchell caught sight of me eying him in the mirror and turned to me. "Something wrong?"

"No. Uh . . . you're Dr. Twitchell, aren't you? At the university?"

"Denver University, yes. Have we met?"

I had almost slipped, having forgotten that he taught at the city university in this year. Remembering in two directions is difficult. "No, Doctor, but I've heard you lecture. You might say I'm one of your fans."

His mouth twitched in a half-smile but he did not rise to it. From that and other things I learned that he had not yet acquired a gnawing need for adulation; he was sure of himself at that age and needed only his own self-approval. "Are you sure you haven't got me mixed up with a movie star?"

"Oh no! You're Dr. Hubert Twitchell . . . the great physicist."

His mouth twitched again. "Let's just say that I am a physicist. Or try to be."

We chatted for a while and I tried to hang onto him after he had finished his sandwich. I said it would be an honor if he would let me buy him a drink. He shook his head. "I hardly drink at all and certainly never before dark. Thanks anyway. It's been nice meeting you. Drop into my lab someday if you are ever around the campus."

I said I would.

But I did not make many slips in 1970 (second time around) because I understood it and, anyhow, most people who might have recognized me were in California. I resolved that if I did meet any more familiar faces I would give them the cold stare and the quick brushoff—take no chances.

But little things can cause you trouble too. Like the time I got caught in a zipper simply because I had become used to the more convenient and much safer Sticktite closures. A lot of little things like that I missed very much after having learned in only six months to take them for granted. Shaving—I had to go back to *shaving!* Once I even caught a cold. That horrid ghost of the past resulted from forgetting that clothes could get soaked in rain. I wish that those precious esthetes who sneer at progress and prattle about the superior beauties of the past could have been with me—dishes that let food get chilled, shirts that had to be laundered, bathroom mirrors that steamed up when you needed them, runny noses, dirt underfoot and dirt in your lungs—I had become used to a better way of living and 1970 was a series of petty frustrations until I got the hang of it again.

But a dog gets used to his fleas and so did I. Denver in 1970 was a very quaint place with a fine old-fashioned flavor; I became very fond of it. It was nothing like the slick New Plan maze it had been (or would be) when I had arrived (or would arrive) there from Yuma; it still had less than two million people, there were still busses and other vehicular traffic in the streets—there still were *streets;* I had no trouble finding Colfax Avenue.

Denver was still getting used to being the national seat of government and was not quite happy in the role, like a boy in his first formal evening clothes. Its spirit still yearned for high-heeled boots and its western twang even though it knew it had to grow up and be an international metropolis, with embassies and spies and famous gourmet restaurants. The city was being jerry-built in all directions to house the bureaucrats and lobbyists and contact men and clerk-typists and flunkies; buildings were being thrown up so fast that with each one there was hazard of enclosing a cow inside the walls. Nevertheless, the city had extended only a few miles past Aurora on the east, to Henderson on the north, and Littleton on the south—there was still open country before you reached the Air Academy. On the west, of course, the city flowed into the high country and the federal bureaus were tunneling back into the mountains.

I liked Denver during its federal boom. Nevertheless, I was excruciatingly anxious to get back to my own time.

It was always the little things. I had had my teeth worked over completely shortly after I had been put on the staff of Hired Girl and could afford it. I had never expected to have to see a dental plastician again. Nevertheless, in 1970 I did not have anti-caries pills and so I got a hole in a tooth, a painful one or I would have ignored it. So I went to a dentist. So help me, I had forgotten what he would see when he looked into my mouth. He blinked, moved his mirror around, and said, "Great jumping Jehosaphat! Who was your dentist?"

"Kah hoo hank?"

He took his hands out of my mouth. "Who did it? And how?"

"Huh? You mean my teeth? Oh, that's experimental work they're doing in . . . India."

"How do they do it?"

"How would I know?"

"Mmm . . . wait a minute. I've got to get some pictures of this." He started fiddling with his X-ray equipment.

"Oh no," I objected. "Just clean out that bicuspid, plug it up with anything, and let me out of here."

"But——"

"I'm sorry, Doctor. But I'm on a dead run."

So he did as I said, pausing now and again to look at my teeth. I paid cash and did not leave my name. I suppose I could have let him have the pics, but covering up had become a reflex. It couldn't have hurt anything to let him have them. Nor helped either, as X rays would not show how regeneration was accomplished, nor could I have told him.

There is no time like the past to get things done. While I was sweating sixteen hours a day on *Drafting Dan* and *Protean Pete* I got something else done with my left hand. Working anonymously through John's law office I hired a detective agency with national branches to dig up Belle's past. I supplied them with her address and the license number and model of her car (since steering wheels are good places to get fingerprints) and suggested that she might have been married here and there and possibly might have a police record. I had to limit the budget severely; I couldn't afford the sort of investigation you read about.

When they did not report back in ten days I kissed my money good-by. But a few days later a thick envelope showed up at John's office.

Belle had been a busy girl. Born six years earlier than she claimed, she had been married twice before she was eighteen. One of them did not count because the man already had a wife;

if she had been divorced from the second the agency had not uncovered it.

She had apparently been married four times since then, although once was doubtful; it may have been the "war-widow" racket worked with the aid of a man who was dead and could not object. She had been divorced once (respondent) and one of her husbands was dead. She might still be "married" to the others.

Her police record was long and interesting but apparently she had been convicted of a felony only once, in Nebraska, and granted parole without doing time. This was established only by fingerprints, as she had jumped parole, changed her name, and had acquired a new social-security number. The agency asked if they were to notify Nebraska authorities.

I told them not to bother; she had been missing for nine years and her conviction had been for nothing worse than lure in a badger game. I wondered what I would have done if it had been dope peddling? Reflexive decisions have their complications.

I ran behind schedule on the drawings and October was on me before I knew it. I still had the descriptions only half worded, since they had to tie into drawings, and I had done nothing about the claims. Worse, I had done nothing about organizing the deal so that it would hold up; I could not do it until I had a completed job to show. Nor had I had time to make contacts. I began to think that I had made a mistake in not asking Dr. Twitchell to set the controls for at least thirty-two years instead of thirty-one years and a fiddling three weeks; I had underestimated the time I would need and overestimated my own capacity.

I had not shown my toys to my friends, the Suttons, not because I wanted to hide them, but because I had not wanted a lot of talk and useless advice while they were incomplete. On the last Saturday in September I was scheduled to go out to the club camp with them. Being behind schedule, I had worked late the night before, then had been awakened early by the torturing clang of an alarm clock so that I could shave and be ready to go when they came by. I shut the sadistic thing off and thanked God that they had got rid of such horrible devices in 2001, then I pulled myself groggily together and went down to the corner drugstore to phone and say that I couldn't make it, I had to work.

Jenny answered, "Danny, you're working too hard. A weekend in the country will do you good."

"I can't help it, Jenny. I have to. I'm sorry."

John got on the other phone and said, "What's all this nonsense?"

"I've got to work, John. I've simply got to. Say hello to the folks for me."

I went back upstairs, burned some toast, vulcanized some eggs, sat back down at *Drafting Dan*.

An hour later they banged on my door.

None of us went to the mountains that weekend. Instead I demonstrated both devices. Jenny was not much impressed by *Drafting Dan* (it isn't a woman's gismo, unless she herself is an engineer), but she was wide-eyed over *Protean Pete*. She kept house with a Mark II *Hired Girl* and could see how much more this machine could do.

But John could see the importance of *Drafting Dan*. When I showed him how I could write my signature, recognizably my own, just by punching keys—I admit I had practiced—his eyebrows stayed up. "Chum, you're going to throw draftsmen out of work by the thousand."

"No, I won't. The shortage of engineering talent in this country gets worse every year; this gadget will just help to fill the gap. In a generation you are going to see this tool in every engineering and architectural office in the nation. They'll be as lost without it as a modern mechanic would be without power tools."

"You talk as if you knew."

"I do know."

He looked over at *Protean Pete*—I had set him to tidying my workbench—and back at *Drafting Dan*. "Danny . . . sometimes I think maybe you were telling me the truth, you know, the day we met you."

I shrugged. "Call it second sight . . . but I do know. I'm certain. Does it matter?"

"I guess not. What are your plans for these things?"

I frowned. "That's the hitch, John. I'm a good engineer and a fair jackleg mechanic when I have to be. But I'm no businessman; I've proved that. You've never fooled with patent law?"

"I told you that before. It's a job for a specialist."

"Do you know an honest one? Who's smart as a whip besides? It's reached the point where I've got to have one. I've got to set up a corporation, too, to handle it. And work out the financing. But I haven't got much time; I'm *terribly* pressed for time."

"Why?"

"I'm going back where I came from."

He sat and said nothing for quite a while. At last he said, "How much time?"

"Uh, about nine weeks. Nine weeks from this coming Thursday to be exact."

He looked at the two machines, looked back at me. "Better revise your schedule. I'd say that you had more like nine months' work cut out for you. You won't be in production even then—just lined up to start moving, with luck."

"John, I can't!"

"I'll say you can't."

"I mean I can't change my schedule. That's beyond my control . . . now." I put my face in my hands. I was dead with fatigue, having had less than five hours' sleep and having averaged not much better for days. The shape I was in, I was willing to believe that there was something, after all, to this "fate" business—a man could struggle against it but never beat it.

I looked up. "Will *you* handle it?"

"Eh? What part of it?"

"Everything. I've done all I know how to do."

"That's a big order, Dan. I could rob you blind. You know that, don't you? And this may be a gold mine."

"It will be. I know."

"Then why trust me? You had better just keep me as your attorney, advice for a fee."

I tried to think while my head ached. I had taken a partner once before—but, damnation, no matter how many times you get your fingers burned, you *have* to trust people. Otherwise you are a hermit in a cave, sleeping with one eye open. There wasn't any way to be safe; just being alive was deadly dangerous . . . fatal, in the end.

"Cripes, John, you know the answer to that. *You* trusted *me*. Now I need your help again. Will you help me?"

"Of course he will," Jenny put in gently, "though I haven't

heard what you two were talking about. Danny? Can it wash dishes? Every dish you have is dirty."

"What, Jenny? Why, I suppose he can. Yes, of course he can."

"Then tell him to, please. I want to see it."

"Oh. I've never programmed him for it. I will if you want me to. But it will take several hours to do it right. Of course after that he'll always be able to do it. But the first time . . . well, you see, dishwashing involves a lot of alternate choices. It's a 'judgment' job, not a comparatively simple routine like laying bricks or driving a truck."

"Goodness! I'm certainly glad to find that at least one man understands housework. Did you hear what he said, dear? But don't stop to teach him now, Danny. I'll do them myself." She looked around. "Danny, you've been living like a pig, to put it gently."

To tell the simple truth, it had missed me entirely that *Protean Pete* could work for *me*. I had been engrossed in planning how he could work for other people in commercial jobs, and teaching him to do them, while I myself had simply been sweeping dirt into the corner or ignoring it. Now I began teaching him all the household tasks that *Flexible Frank* had learned; he had the capacity, as I had installed three times as many Thorsen tubes in him as *Frank* had had.

I had time to do it, for John took over.

Jenny typed descriptions for us; John retained a patent attorney to help with the claims. I don't know whether John paid him cash or cut him in on the cake; I never asked. I left the whole thing up to him, including what our shares should be; not only did it leave me free for my proper work, but I figured that if he decided such things he could never be tempted the way Miles had been. And I honestly did not care; money as such is not important. Either John and Jenny were what I thought they were or I might as well find that cave and be a hermit.

I insisted on just two things. "John, I think we ought to call the firm 'The Aladdin Autoengineering Corporation.'"

"Sounds pretty fancy. What's wrong with 'Davis & Sutton'?"

"That's how it's got to be, John."

"So? Is your second sight telling you this?"

"Could be, could be. We'll use a picture of Aladdin rubbing his lamp as a trade-mark, with the genie forming above him. I'll make a rough sketch. And one other thing: the home office had better be in Los Angeles."

"What? Now you've gone too far. That is, if you expect me to run it. What's wrong with Denver?"

"Nothing is wrong with Denver, it's a nice town. But it is not the place to set up the factory. Pick a good site here and some bright morning you wake up and find that the federal enclave has washed over it and you are out of business until you get re-established on a new one. Besides that, labor is scarce, raw materials come overland, building materials are all gray-market. Whereas Los Angeles has an unlimited supply of skilled workmen and more pouring in every day, Los Angeles is a seaport, Los Angeles is——"

"How about the smog? It's not worth it."

"They'll lick the smog before long. Believe me. And haven't you noticed that Denver is working up smog of its own?"

"Now wait a minute, Dan. You've already made it clear that I will have to run this while you go kiyoodling off on some business of your own. Okay, I agreed. But I ought to have some choice in working conditions."

"It's necessary, John."

"Dan, nobody in his right mind who lives in Colorado would move to California. I was stationed out there during the war; I *know*. Take Jenny here; she's a native Californian, that's her secret shame. You couldn't hire her to go back. Here you've got winters, changing seasons, brisk mountain air, magnificent——"

Jenny looked up. "Oh, I wouldn't go so far as to say I'd *never* go back."

"What's that, dear?"

Jenny had been quietly knitting; she never talked unless she really had something to say. Now she put down her knitting, a clear sign. "If we did move there, dear, we could join the Oakdale Club; they have outdoor swimming all year round. I was thinking of that just this last weekend when I saw ice on the pool at Boulder."

I stayed until the evening of 2 December, 1970, the last possible minute. I was forced to borrow three thousand dollars from John—the prices I had paid for components had been scandalous

—but I offered him a stock mortgage to secure it. He let me sign it, then tore it up and dropped it in a wastebasket. "Pay me when you get around to it."

"It will be thirty years, John."

"As long as that?"

I pondered it. He had never invited me to tell my whole story since the afternoon, six months earlier, when he had told me frankly that he did not believe the essential part—but was going to vouch for me to their club anyhow.

I told him I thought it was time to tell him. "Shall we wake up Jenny? She's entitled to hear it too."

"Mmm . . . no. Let her nap until just before you have to leave. Jenny is a very uncomplicated person, Dan. She doesn't care who you are or where you came from as long as she likes you. If it seems a good idea, I can pass it on to her later."

"As you will." He let me tell it all, stopping only to fill our glasses—mine with ginger ale; I had a reason not to touch alcohol. When I had brought it up to the point where I landed on a mountainside outside Boulder, I stopped. "That's it," I said. "Though I was mixed up on one point. I've looked at the contour since and I don't think my fall was more than two feet. If they had—I mean 'if they were going to'—bulldoze that laboratory site any deeper, I would have been buried alive. Probably would have killed both of you too—if it didn't blow up the whole county. I don't know just what happens when a flat wave form changes back into a mass where another mass already is."

John went on smoking. "Well?" I said. "What do you think?"

"Danny, you've told me a lot of things about what Los Angeles —I mean 'Great Los Angeles'—is going to be like. I'll let you know when I see you just how accurate you've been."

"It's accurate. Subject to minor slips of memory."

"Mmm . . . you certainly make it sound logical. But in the meantime I think you are the most agreeable lunatic I've ever met. Not that it handicaps you as an engineer . . . or as a friend. I like you, boy. I'm going to buy you a new strait jacket for Christmas."

"Have it your own way."

"I *have* to have it this way. The alternative is that I myself am stark staring mad . . . and that would make quite a problem for

Jenny." He glanced at the clock. "We'd better wake her. She'd scalp me if I let you leave without saying good-by to her."

"I wouldn't think of it."

They drove me to Denver International Port and Jenny kissed me good-by at the gate. I caught the eleven o'clock shuttle for Los Angeles.

XI

The following evening, 3 December, 1970, I had a cabdriver drop me a block from Miles's house comfortably early, as I did not know exactly what time I had arrived there the first time. It was already dark as I approached his house, but I saw only his car at the curb, so I backed off a hundred yards to a spot where I could watch that stretch of curb and waited.

Two cigarettes later I saw another car pull up there, stop, and its lights go out. I waited a couple of minutes longer, then hurried toward it. It was my own car.

I did not have a key but that was no hurdle; I was always getting ears-deep in an engineering problem and forgetting my keys; I had long ago formed the habit of keeping a spare ditched in the trunk. I got it now and climbed into the car. I had parked on a slight grade heading downhill, so, without turning on lights or starting the engine, I let it drift to the corner and turned there, then switched on the engine but not the lights, and parked again in the alley back of Miles's house and on which his garage faced.

The garage was locked. I peered through dirty glass and saw a shape with a sheet over it. By its contours I knew it was my old friend *Flexible Frank.*

Garage doors are not built to resist a man armed with a tire iron and determination—not in southern California in 1970. It took seconds. Carving *Frank* into pieces I could carry and stuff into my car took much longer. But first I checked to see that the notes and drawings were where I suspected they were—they were indeed, so I hauled them out and dumped them on the floor of the car, then tackled *Frank* himself. Nobody knew as well as I did how he was put together, and it speeded up things enormously that I did not care how much damage I did; nevertheless, I was as busy as a one-man band for nearly an hour.

I had just stowed the last piece, the wheel-chair chassis, in the car trunk and had lowered the turtleback down on it as far as it would go when I heard Pete start to wail. Swearing to myself at the time it had taken to tear *Frank* apart, I hurried around the garage and into their back yard. Then the commotion started.

I had promised myself that I would relish every second of Pete's triumph. But I couldn't see it. The back door was open and light was streaming out the screen door, but while I could hear sounds of running, crashes, Pete's blood-chilling war cry, and screams from Belle, they never accommodated me by coming into my theater of vision. So I crept up to the screen door, hoping to catch a glimpse of the carnage.

The damned thing was hooked! It was the only thing that had failed to follow the schedule. So I frantically dug into my pocket, broke a nail getting my knife open—and jabbed through and unhooked it just in time to jump out of the way as Pete hit the screen like a stunt motorcyclist hitting a fence.

I fell over a rosebush. I don't know whether Miles and Belle even tried to follow him outside. I doubt it; I would not have risked it in their spot. But I was too busy getting myself untangled to notice.

Once I was on my feet I stayed behind bushes and moved around to the side of the house; I wanted to get away from that open door and the light pouring out of it. Then it was just a case of waiting until Pete quieted down. I would not touch him then, certainly not try to pick him up. I know cats.

But every time he passed me, prowling for an entrance and sounding his deep challenge, I called out to him softly. "Pete. Come here, Pete. Easy, boy, it's all right."

He knew I was there and twice he looked at me, but otherwise ignored me. With cats it is one thing at a time; he had urgent business right now and no time to head-bump with Papa. But I knew he would come to me when his emotions had eased off.

While I squatted, waiting, I heard water running in their bathrooms and guessed that they had gone to clean up, leaving me in the living room. I had a horrid thought then: what would happen if I sneaked in and cut the throat of my own helpless body? But I suppressed it; I wasn't that curious and suicide is such a final experiment, even if the circumstances are mathematically intriguing.

But I never have figured it out.

Besides, I didn't want to go inside for any purpose. I might run into Miles—and I didn't want any truck with a dead man.

Pete finally stopped in front of me about three feet out of reach. "Mrrrowrr?" he said—meaning, "Let's go back and clean out the joint. You hit 'em high, I'll hit 'em low."

"No, boy. The show is over."

"Aw, c'mahnnn!"

"Time to go home, Pete. Come to Danny."

He sat down and started to wash himself. When he looked up, I put my arms out and he jumped into them. "Kwleert?" ("Where the hell were *you* when the riot started?")

I carried him back to the car and dumped him in the driver's space, which was all there was left. He sniffed the hardware on his accustomed place and looked around reproachfully. "You'll have to sit in my lap," I said. "Quit being fussy."

I switched on the car's lights as we hit the street. Then I turned east and headed for Big Bear and the Girl Scout camp. I chucked away enough of *Frank* in the first ten minutes to permit Pete to resume his rightful place, which suited us both better. When I had the floor clear, several miles later, I stopped and shoved the notes and drawings down a storm drain. The wheel-chair chassis I did not get rid of until we were actually in the mountains, then it went down a deep arroyo, making a nice sound effect.

About three in the morning I pulled into a motor court across the road and down a bit from the turnoff into the Girl Scout camp, and paid too much for a cabin—Pete almost queered it by sticking his head up and making a comment when the owner came out.

"What time," I asked him, "does the morning mail from Los Angeles get up here?"

"Helicopter comes in at seven-thirteen, right on the dot."

"Fine. Give me a call at seven, will you?"

"Mister, if you can sleep as late as seven around here you're better than I am. But I'll put you in the book."

By eight o'clock Pete and I had eaten breakfast and I had showered and shaved. I looked Pete over in daylight and concluded that he had come through the battle undamaged except for possibly a bruise or two. We checked out and I drove into the private road for the camp. Uncle Sam's truck turned in just ahead of me; I decided that it was my day.

I never saw so many little girls in my life. They skittered like kittens and they all looked alike in their green uniforms. Those I passed wanted to look at Pete, though most of them just stared shyly and did not approach. I went to a cabin marked "Headquarters," where I spoke to another uniformed scout who was decidedly no longer a girl.

She was properly suspicious of me; strange men who want to be allowed to visit little girls just turning into big girls should always be suspected.

I explained that I was the child's uncle, Daniel B. Davis by name, and that I had a message for the child concerning her family. She countered with the statement that visitors other than parents were permitted only when accompanied by a parent and, in any case, visiting hours were not until four o'clock.

"I don't want to visit with Frederica, but I must give her this message. It's an emergency."

"In that case you can write it out and I will give it to her as soon as she is through with rhythm games."

I looked upset (and was) and said, "I don't want to do that. It would be much kinder to tell the child in person."

"Death in the family?"

"Not quite. Family trouble, yes. I'm sorry, ma'am, but I am not free to tell anyone else. It concerns my niece's mother."

She was weakening but still undecided. Then Pete joined the discussion. I had been carrying him with his bottom in the crook of my left arm and his chest supported with my right hand; I had not wanted to leave him in the car and I knew Ricky would want to see him. He'll put up with being carried that way quite a while but now he was getting bored. "Krrwarr?"

She looked at him and said, "He's a fine boy, that one. I have a tabby at home who could have come from the same litter."

I said solemnly, "He's Frederica's cat. I had to bring him along because . . . well, it was necessary. No one to take care of him."

"Oh, the poor little fellow!" She scratched him under the chin, doing it properly, thank goodness, and Pete accepted it, thank goodness again, stretching his neck and closing his eyes and looking indecently pleased. He is capable of taking a very stiff line with strangers if he does not fancy their overtures.

The guardian of youth told me to sit down at a table under the trees outside the headquarters. It was far enough away to permit a private visit but still under her careful eye. I thanked her and waited.

I didn't see Ricky come up. I heard a shout, "Uncle Danny!" and another one as I turned, "And you brought *Pete!* Oh, this is *wonderful!*"

Pete gave a long bubbling *bleerrrt* and leaped from my arms to hers. She caught him neatly, rearranged him in the support position he likes best, and they ignored me for a few seconds while exchanging cat protocols. Then she looked up and said soberly, "Uncle Danny, I'm awful glad you're here."

I didn't kiss her; I did not touch her at all. I've never been one to paw children and Ricky was the sort of little girl who only put up with it when she could not avoid it. Our original relationship, back when she was six, had been founded on mutual decent respect for the other's individualism and personal dignity.

But I did look at her. Knobby knees, stringy, shooting up fast, not yet filled out, she was not as pretty as she had been as a baby girl. The shorts and T-shirt she was wearing, combined with peeling sunburn, scratches, bruises, and an understandable amount of dirt, did not add up to feminine glamour. She was a matchstick sketch of the woman she would become, her coltish gawkiness relieved only by her enormous solemn eyes and the pixie beauty of her thin smudged features.

She looked adorable.

I said, "And I'm awful glad to be here, Ricky."

Trying awkwardly to manage Pete with one arm, she reached with her other hand for a bulging pocket in her shorts. "I'm surprised too. I just this minute got a letter from you—they dragged me away from mail call; I haven't even had a chance to open it. Does it say that you're coming today?" She got it out, creased and mussed from being crammed into a pocket too small.

"No, it doesn't, Ricky. It says I'm going away. But after I mailed it, I decided I just had to come say good-by in person."

She looked bleak and dropped her eyes. "You're going away?"

"Yes. I'll explain, Ricky, but it's rather long. Let's sit down and I'll tell you about it." So we sat on opposite sides of the picnic table under the ponderosas and I talked. Pete lay on the table between us, making a library lion of himself with his fore-paws on the creased letter, and sang a low song like bees buzzing in deep clover, while he narrowed his eyes in contentment.

I was much relieved to find that she already knew that Miles had married Belle—I hadn't relished having to break that to her. She glanced up, dropped her eyes at once, and said with no expression at all, "Yes, I know. Daddy wrote me about it."

"Oh. I see."

She suddenly looked grim and not at all a child. "I'm not going back there, Danny. I *won't* go back there."

"But—— Look here, Rikki-tikki-tavi, I know how you feel. I certainly don't want you to go back there—I'd take you away myself if I could. But how can you help going back? He's your daddy and you are only eleven."

"I don't have to go back. He's not my real daddy. My grandmother is coming to get me."

"What? When's she coming?"

"Tomorrow. She has to drive up from Brawley. I wrote her about it and asked her if I could come live with her because I wouldn't live with Daddy any more with *her* there." She managed to put more contempt into one pronoun than an adult could have squeezed out of profanity. "Grandma wrote back and said that I didn't have to live there if I didn't want to because he had never adopted me and she was my 'guardian of record.'" She looked up anxiously. "That's right, isn't it? They can't make me?"

I felt an overpowering flood of relief. The one thing I had not been able to figure out, a problem that had worried me for months, was how to keep Ricky from being subjected to the poisonous in-fluence of Belle for—well, two years; it had seemed certain that it would be about two years. "If he never adopted you, Ricky, I'm certain that your grandmother can make it stick if you are both firm about it." Then I frowned and chewed my lip. "But you may have some trouble tomorrow. They may object to letting you go with her."

"How can they stop me? I'll just get in the car and go."

"It's not that simple, Ricky. These people who run the camp, they have to follow rules. Your daddy—Miles, I mean—Miles turned you over to them; they won't be willing to turn you back over to anyone but him."

She stuck out her lower lip. "I won't go. I'm going with Grandma."

"Yes. But maybe I can tell you how to make it easy. If I were you, I wouldn't tell them that I'm leaving camp; I'd just tell them that your grandmother wants to take you for a ride—then don't come back."

Some of her tension relaxed. "All right."

"Uh . . . don't pack a bag or anything or they may guess what you're doing. Don't try to take any clothes but those you are wearing at the time. Put any money or anything you really want to save into your pockets. You don't have much here that you would really mind losing, I suppose?"

"I guess not." But she looked wistful. "I've got a brand-new swim suit."

How do you explain to a child that there are times when you just must abandon your baggage? You can't—they'll go back into a burning building to save a doll or a toy elephant. "Mmm . . . Ricky, have your grandmother tell them that she is taking you over to Arrowhead to have a swim with her . . . and that she may take you to dinner at the hotel there, but that she will have you back before taps. Then you can carry your swimming suit and a towel. But nothing else. Er, will your grandmother tell that fib for you?"

"I guess so. Yes, I'm sure she will. She says people have to tell little white fibs or else people couldn't stand each other. But she says fibs were meant to be used, not abused."

"She sounds like a sensible person. You'll do it that way?"

"I'll do it just that way, Danny."

"Good." I picked up the battered envelope. "Ricky, I told you I had to go away. I have to go away for a very long time."

"How long?"

"Thirty years."

Her eyes grew wider if possible. At eleven, thirty years is not a long time; it's forever. I added, "I'm sorry, Ricky. But I have to."

"Why?"

I could not answer that one. The true answer was unbelievable and a lie would not do. "Ricky, it's much too hard to explain. But I have to. I can't help it." I hesitated, then added, "I'm going to take the Long Sleep. The cold sleep—you know what I mean."

She knew. Children get used to new ideas faster than adults do; cold sleep was a favorite comic-book theme. She looked horrified and protested, "But, Danny, I'll *never see you again!*"

"Yes, you will. It's a long time but I'll see you again. And so will Pete. Because Pete is going with me; he's going to cold-sleep too."

She glanced at Pete and looked more woebegone than ever. "But—— Danny, why don't you and Pete just come down to Brawley and live with us? That would be ever so much better. Grandma will like Pete. She'll like you too—she says there's nothing like having a man around the house."

"Ricky . . . dear Ricky . . . I *have* to. Please don't tease me." I started to tear open the envelope.

She looked angry and her chin started to quiver. "I think *she* has something to do with this!"

"What? If you mean Belle, she doesn't. Not exactly, anyway."

"She's not going to cold-sleep with you?"

I think I shuddered. "Good heavens, no! I'd run miles to avoid her."

Ricky seemed slightly mollified. "You know, I was so *mad* at you about *her*. I had an awful outrage."

"I'm sorry, Ricky. I'm truly sorry. You were right and I was wrong. But she hasn't anything to do with this. I'm through with her, forever and forever and cross my heart. Now about this." I held up the certificate for all that I owned in Hired Girl, Inc. "Do you know what it is?"

"No."

I explained it to her. "I'm giving this to you, Ricky. Because I'm going to be gone so long I want you to have it." I took the paper on which I had written an assignment to her, tore it up, and put the pieces in my pocket; I could not risk doing it that way—it would be too easy for Belle to tear up a separate sheet and we were not yet out of the woods. I turned the certificate over and studied the standard assignment form on the back, trying to plan how to word it in the spaces provided. I finally squeezed in an assignment to the Bank of America in trust for——

"Ricky, what is your full name?"

"Frederica Virginia. Frederica Virginia Gentry. You know."

"Is it 'Gentry'? I thought you said Miles had never adopted you?"

"Oh! I've been Ricky Gentry as long as I can remember. But you mean my *real* name. It's the same as Grandma's . . . the same as my real daddy's. Heinicke. But nobody ever calls me that."

"They will now." I wrote "Frederica Virginia Heinicke" and added "and to be reassigned to her on her twenty-first birthday" while prickles ran down my spine—my original assignment might have been defective in any case.

I started to sign and then noticed our watchdog sticking her head out of the office. I glanced at my wrist, saw that we had been talking an hour; I was running out of minutes.

But I wanted it nailed down tight. "Ma'am!"

"Yes?"

"By any chance, is there a notary public around here? Or must I find one in the village?"

"I am a notary. What do you wish?"

"Oh, good! Wonderful! Do you have your seal?"

"I never go anywhere without it."

So I signed my name under her eye and she even stretched a point (on Ricky's assurance that she knew me and Pete's silent testimony to my respectability as a fellow member of the fraternity of cat people) and used the long form: "—known to me personally as being said Daniel B. Davis——" When she embossed her seal through my signature and her own I sighed with relief. Just let Belle try to find a way to twist that one!

She glanced at it curiously but said nothing. I said solemnly, "Tragedies cannot be undone but this will help. The kid's education, you know."

She refused a fee and went back into the office. I turned back

176

to Ricky and said, "Give this to your grandmother. Tell her to take it to a branch of the Bank of America in Brawley. They'll do everything else." I laid it in front of her.

She did not touch it. "That's worth a lot of money, isn't it?"

"Quite a bit. It will be worth more."

"I don't want it."

"But, Ricky, I want you to have it."

"I don't want it. I won't *take* it." Her eyes filled with tears and her voice got unsteady. "You're going away forever and . . . and you don't care about me any more." She sniffed. "Just like when you got engaged to *her*. When you could just as easily bring Pete and come live with Grandma and me. I don't *want* your money!"

"Ricky. Listen to me, Ricky. It's too late. I couldn't take it back now if I wanted to. It's already yours."

"I don't care. I won't ever touch it." She reached out and stroked Pete. "Pete wouldn't go away and leave me . . . only you're going to make him. Now I won't even have Pete."

I answered unsteadily, "Ricky? Rikki-tikki-tavi? You want to see Pete . . . and me again?"

I could hardly hear her. "Of course I do. But I won't."

"But you can."

"Huh? How? You said you were going to take the Long Sleep . . . thirty years, you said."

"And I am. I have to. But, Ricky, here is what you can do. Be a good girl, go live with your grandmama, go to school—and just let this money pile up. When you are twenty-one—if you still want to see us—you'll have enough money to take the Long Sleep yourself. When you wake up I'll be there waiting for you. Pete and I will both be waiting for you. That's a solemn promise."

Her expression changed but she did not smile. She thought about it quite a long time, then said, "You'll really be there?"

"Yes. But we'll have to make a date. If you do it, Ricky, do it just the way I tell you. You arrange it with the Cosmopolitan Insurance Company and you make sure that you take your Sleep in the Riverside Sanctuary in Riverside . . . and you make very sure that they have orders to wake you up on the first day of May, 2001, exactly. I'll be there that day, waiting for you. If you want me to be there when you first open your eyes, you'll have to leave word for that, too, or they won't let me farther than the waiting room—I know that sanctuary; they're very fussy." I took out an envelope which I had prepared before I left Denver. "You don't have to remember this; I've got it all written out for you. Just save it, and on your twenty-first birthday you can make up your mind. But you can be sure that Pete and I will be there waiting for you, whether you show up or not." I laid the prepared instructions on the stock certificate.

I thought that I had her convinced but she did not touch either of them. She stared at them, then presently said, "Danny?"

"Yes, Ricky?"

She would not look up and her voice was so low that I could barely hear her. But I did hear her. "If I do . . . will you marry me?"

My ears roared and the lights flickered. But I answered steadily and much louder than she had spoken. "Yes, Ricky. That's what I want. That's why I'm doing this."

I had just one more thing to leave with her: a prepared envelope marked "To Be Opened in the Event of the Death of Miles Gentry." I did not explain it to her; I just told her to keep it. It contained proof of Belle's varied career, matrimonial and otherwise. In the hands of a lawyer it should make a court fight over his will no contest at all.

Then I gave her my class ring from Tech (it was all I had) and told her it was hers; we were engaged. "It's too big for you but you can keep it. I'll have another one for you when you wake up."

She held it tight in her fist. "I won't want another one."

"All right. Now better tell Pete good-by, Ricky. I've got to go. I can't wait a minute longer."

She hugged Pete, then handed him back to me, looked me steadily in the eye even though tears were running down her nose and leaving clean streaks. "Good-by, Danny."

"Not 'good-by,' Ricky. Just 'so long.' We'll be waiting for you."

It was a quarter of ten when I got back to the village. I found that a helicopter bus was due to leave for the center of the city in twenty-five minutes, so I sought out the only used-car lot and made one of the fastest deals in history, letting my car go for half what it was worth for cash in hand at once. It left me just time to sneak Pete into the bus (they are fussy about airsick cats) and we reached Powell's office just after eleven o'clock.

Powell was much annoyed that I had canceled my arrangements for Mutual to handle my estate and was especially inclined to lecture me over having lost my papers. "I can't very well ask the same judge to pass on your committal twice in the same twenty-four hours. It's most irregular."

I waved money at him, cash money with convincing figures on it. "Never mind eating me out about it, Sergeant. Do you want my business or don't you? If not, say so, and I'll beat it on up to Central Valley. Because I'm going today."

He still fumed but he gave in. Then he grumbled about adding six months to the cold-sleep period and did not want to guarantee an exact date of awakening. "The contracts ordinarily read 'plus or minus' one month to allow for administrative hazards."

"This one doesn't. This one reads 27 April, 2001. But I don't care whether it says 'Mutual' at the top or 'Central Valley.' Mr. Powell, I'm buying and you're selling. If you don't sell what I want to buy I'll go where they do sell it."

He changed the contract and we both initialed it.

At twelve straight up I was back in for my final check with their medical examiner. He looked at me. "Did you stay sober?"

"Sober as a judge."

"That's no recommendation. We'll see." He went over me almost as carefully as he had "yesterday." At last he put down his rubber hammer and said, "I'm surprised. You're in much better shape than you were yesterday. Amazingly so."

"Doc, you don't know the half of it."

I held Pete and soothed him while they gave him the first sedative. Then I lay back myself and let them work on me. I suppose I could have waited another day, or even longer, just as well as not—but the truth was that I was frantically anxious to get back to 2001.

About four in the afternoon, with Pete's flat head resting on my chest, I went happily to sleep again.

XII

My dreams were pleasanter this time. The only bad one I remember was not too bad, but simply endless frustration. It was a cold dream in which I wandered shivering through branching corridors, trying every door I came to, thinking that the next one would surely be the Door into Summer, with Ricky waiting on the other side. I was hampered by Pete, "following me ahead of me," that exasperating habit cats have of scalloping back and forth between the legs of persons trusted not to step on them or kick them.

At each new door he would duck between my feet, look out it, find it still winter outside, and reverse himself, almost tripping me.

But neither one of us gave up his conviction that the next door would be the right one.

I woke up easily this time, with no disorientation—in fact the doctor was somewhat irked that all I wanted was some breakfast, the Great Los Angeles *Times*, and no chitchat. I didn't think it was worth while to explain to him that this was my second time around; he would not have believed me.

There was a note waiting for me, dated a week earlier, from John:

Dear Dan,

All right, I give up. How did you do it?

I'm complying with your request not to be met, against Jenny's wishes. She sends her love and hopes that you won't be too long in looking us up—I've tried to explain to her that you expect to be busy for a while. We are both fine although I tend to walk where I used to run. Jenny is even more beautiful than she used to be.

Hasta la vista, amigo,
John

P.S. If the enclosure is not enough, just phone—there is plenty more where it came from. We've done pretty well, I think.

I considered calling John, both to say hello and to tell him about a colossal new idea I had had while asleep—a gadget to change bathing from a chore to a sybaritic delight. But I decided not to; I had other things on my mind. So I made notes while the notion was fresh and then got some sleep, with Pete's head tucked into my armpit. I wish I could cure him of that. It's flattering but a nuisance.

On Monday, the thirtieth of April, I checked out and went over to Riverside, where I got a room in the old Mission Inn. They made the predictable fuss about taking a cat into a room and an autobellhop is not responsive to bribes—hardly an improvement. But the assistant manager had more flexibility in his synapses; he listened to reason as long as it was crisp and rustled. I did not sleep well; I was too excited.

I presented myself to the director of the Riverside Sanctuary at ten o'clock the next morning. "Dr. Rumsey, my name is Daniel B. Davis. You have a committed client here named Frederica Heinicke?"

"I suppose you can identify yourself?"

I showed him a 1970 driver's license issued in Denver, and my withdrawal certificate from Forest Lawn Sanctuary. He looked them over and me, and handed them back. I said anxiously, "I think she's scheduled for withdrawal today. By any chance, are there any instructions to permit me to be present? I don't mean the processing routines; I mean at the last minute, when she's ready for the final restimulant and consciousness."

He shoved his lips out and looked judicial. "Our instructions for this client do not read to wake her today."

"No?" I felt disappointed and hurt.

"No. Her exact wishes are as follows: instead of necessarily being waked today, she wished not to be waked at all until you showed up." He looked me over and smiled. "You must have a heart of gold. I can't account for it on your beauty."

I sighed. "Thanks, Doctor."

"You can wait in the lobby or come back. We won't need you for a couple of hours."

I went back to the lobby, got Pete, and took him for a walk. I had parked him there in his new travel bag and he was none too pleased with it, even though I had bought one as much like his old one as possible and had installed a one-way window in it the night before. It probably didn't smell right as yet.

We passed the "real nice place," but I was not hungry even though I hadn't been able to eat much breakfast—Pete had eaten my eggs and had turned up his nose at yeast strips. At eleven-thirty I was back at the sanctuary. Finally they let me in to see her.

All I could see was her face; her body was covered. But it was my Ricky, grown woman size and looking like a slumbering angel.

"She's under posthypnotic instruction," Dr. Rumsey said softly. "If you will stand just there, I'll bring her up. Uh, I think you had better put that cat outside."

"No, Doctor."

He started to speak, shrugged, turned back to his patient. "Wake up, Frederica. Wake up. You must wake up now."

Her eyelids fluttered, she opened her eyes. They wandered for an instant, then she caught sight of us and smiled sleepily. "Danny . . . and Pete." She raised both arms—and I saw that she was wearing my Tech class ring on her left thumb.

Pete chirrlupped and jumped on the bed, started doing shoulder dives against her in an ecstasy of welcome.

Dr. Rumsey wanted her to stay overnight, but Ricky would have none of it. So I had a cab brought to the door and we jumped to Brawley. Her grandmother had died in 1980 and her social links there had gone by attrition, but she had left things in storage there—books mostly. I ordered them shipped to Aladdin, care of John Sutton. Ricky was a little dazzled by the changes in her old home town and never let go my arm, but she never succumbed to that terrible homesickness which is the great hazard of the Sleep. She merely wanted to get out of Brawley as quickly as possible.

So I hired another cab and we jumped to Yuma. There I signed the county clerk's book in a fine round hand, using my full name "Daniel Boone Davis," so that there could be no possible doubt as to which D. B. Davis had designed this magnum opus. A few minutes later I was standing with her little hand in mine and choking over, "I, Daniel, take thee, Frederica . . . till death us do part."

Pete was my best man. The witnesses we scraped up in the courthouse.

We got out of Yuma at once and jumped to a guest ranch near Tucson, where we had a cabin away from the main lodge and equipped with our own *Eager Beaver* to fetch and carry so that we did not need to see anyone. Pete fought a monumental battle with the tom who until then had been boss of the ranch, whereupon we had to keep Pete in or watch him. This was the only shortcoming I can think of. Ricky took to being married as if she had invented it, and me—well, I had Ricky.

There isn't much more to be said. Voting Ricky's Hired Girl stock—it was still the largest single block—I had McBee eased upstairs to "Research Engineer Emeritus" and put Chuck in as chief engineer. John is boss of Aladdin but keeps threatening to retire —an idle threat. He and I and Jenny control the company, since he was careful to issue preferred stock and to float bonds rather than surrender control. I'm not on the board of either corporation; I don't run them and they compete. Competition is a good idea— Darwin thought well of it.

Me, I'm just the "Davis Engineering Company"—a drafting room, a small shop, and an old machinist who thinks I'm crazy but follows my drawings to exact tolerance. When we finish something I put it out for license.

I had my notes on Twitchell recovered. Then I wrote and told him I had made it and returned via cold sleep . . . and apologized abjectly for having "doubted" him. I asked if he wanted to see the manuscript when I finished. He never answered so I guess he is still sore at me.

But I *am* writing it and I'll put it in all major libraries even if I have to publish at my own expense. I owe him that much. I owe him much more; I owe him for Ricky. And for Pete. I'm going to title it *Unsung Genius*.

Jenny and John look as if they would last forever. Thanks to geriatrics, fresh air, sunshine, exercise, and a mind that never worries, Jenny is prettier than ever at . . . well, sixty-three is my guess. John thinks that I am "merely" clairvoyant and does not want to look at the evidence. Well, how *did* I do it? I tried to explain it to Ricky, but she got upset when I told her that while we were on our honeymoon I was actually and no foolin' also up at Boulder, and that while I was visiting her at the Girl Scout camp I was also lying in a drugged stupor in San Fernando Valley.

She turned white. So I said, "Let's put it hypothetically. It's all logical when you look at it mathematically. Suppose we take a guinea pig—white with brown splotches. We put him in the time cage and kick him back a week. But a week earlier we had already found him there, so at that time we had put him in a pen with himself. Now we've got two guinea pigs . . . although actually it's just one guinea pig, one being the other one a week older. So when you took one of them and kicked him back a week and——"

"Wait a minute! Which one?"

"Which one? Why, there never was but one. You took the one a week younger, of course, because——"

"You said there was just one. Then you said there were two. Then you said the two was just one. But you were going to take one of the two . . . when there was just one——"

"I'm trying to *explain* how two can be just one. If you take the younger——"

"How can you tell which guinea pig is younger when they look just alike?"

"Well, you could cut off the tail of the one you are sending back. Then when it came back you would——"

"Why, Danny, how cruel! Besides, guinea pigs don't have tails."

She seemed to think that proved something. I should never have tried to explain.

But Ricky is not one to fret over things that aren't important. Seeing that I was upset, she said softly, "Come here, dear." She rumpled what hair I have left and kissed me. "One of you is all I want, dearest. Two might be more than I could manage. Tell me one thing—are you glad you waited for me to grow up?"

I did my darnedest to convince her that I was.

But the explanation I tried to give does not explain everything. I missed a point even though I was riding the merry-go-round myself and counting the revolutions. Why didn't I see the notice of my own withdrawal? I mean the second one, in April 2001, not the one in December 2000. I should have; I was there and I used to check those lists. I was awakened (second time) on Friday, 27 April, 2001; it should have been in next morning's *Times*. But I did not see it. I've looked it up since and there it is: "D. B. Davis," in the *Times* for Saturday, 28 April, 2001.

Philosophically, just one line of ink can make a different universe as surely as having the continent of Europe missing. Is the old "branching time streams" and "multiple universes" notion correct? Did I bounce into a different universe, different because I had monkeyed with the setup? Even though I found Ricky and Pete in it? Is there another universe somewhere (or some*when*) in which Pete yowled until he despaired, then wandered off to fend for himself, deserted? And in which Ricky never managed to flee with her grandmother but had to suffer the vindictive wrath of Belle?

One line of fine print isn't enough. I probably fell asleep that night and missed reading my own name, then stuffed the paper down the chute next morning, thinking I had finished with it. I *am* absent-minded, particularly when I'm thinking about a job.

But what would I have done if I *had* seen it? Gone there, met myself—and gone stark mad? No, for if I *had* seen it, I wouldn't have done the things I did afterward—"afterward" for me—which led up to it. Therefore it could never have happened that way. The control is a negative feedback type, with a built-in "fail safe," because the very existence of that line of print depended on my not seeing it; the apparent possibility that I might have seen it is one of the excluded "not possibles" of the basic circuit design.

"There's a divinity that shapes our ends, rough-hew them how we will." Free will and predestination in one sentence and both true. There is only *one* real world, with one past and one future. "As it was in the beginning, is now and ever shall be, world without end, amen." Just *one* . . . but big enough and complicated enough to include free will and time travel and everything else in its linkages and feedbacks and guard circuits. You're allowed to do anything inside the rules . . . but you come back to your own door.

I'm not the only person who has time-traveled. Fort listed too many cases not explainable otherwise and so did Ambrose Bierce. And there were those two ladies in the gardens of the Trianon. I have a hunch, too, that old Doc Twitchell closed that switch oftener than he admitted . . . to say nothing of others who may have learned how in the past or future. But I doubt if much ever comes of it. In my case only three people know and two don't believe me. You can't do much if you do time-travel. As Fort said, you railroad only when it comes time to railroad.

But I can't get Leonard Vincent out of my mind. Was he Leonardo da Vinci? Did he beat his way across the continent and go back with Columbus? The encyclopedia says that his life was such-and-such—but he might have revised the record. I know how that is; I've had to do a little of it. They didn't have social-security numbers, ID cards, nor fingerprints in fifteenth-century Italy; he could have swung it.

But think of him, marooned from everything he was used to, aware of flight, of power, of a million things, trying desperately to picture them so that they could be made—but doomed to frustration because you simply can't do the things we do today without centuries of former art to build on.

Tantalus had it easier.

I've thought about what could be done with time travel commercially if it were declassified—making short jumps, setting up machinery to get back, taking along components. But someday you'd make one jump too many and not be able to set up for your return because it's not time to "railroad." Something simple, like a special alloy, could whip you. And there is that truly awful hazard of not knowing which way you are going. Imagine winding up at the court of Henry VIII with a load of subflexive fasartas intended for the twenty-fifth century. Being becalmed in the horse latitudes would be better.

No, you should never market a gadget until the bugs are out of it.

But I'm not worried about "paradoxes" or "causing anachronisms"—if a thirtieth-century engineer does smooth out the bugs and then sets up transfer stations and trade, it will be because the Builder designed the universe that way. He gave us eyes, two hands, a brain; anything we do with them *can't* be a paradox. He doesn't need busybodies to "enforce" His laws; they enforce themselves. There are no miracles and the word "anachronism" is a semantic blank.

But I don't worry about philosophy any more than Pete does. Whatever the truth about this world, I like it. I've found my Door into Summer and I would not time-travel again for fear of getting off at the wrong station. Maybe my son will, but if he does I will urge him to go forward, not back. "Back" is for emergencies; the future is better than the past. Despite the crapehangers, romanticists, and anti-intellectuals, the world steadily grows better because the human mind, applying itself to environment, *makes* it better. With hands . . . with tools . . . with horse sense and science and engineering.

Most of these long-haired belittlers can't drive a nail nor use a slide rule. I'd like to invite them into Dr. Twitchell's cage and ship them back to the twelfth century—then let them enjoy it.

But I am not mad at anybody and I like now. Except that Pete is getting older, a little fatter, and not as inclined to choose a younger opponent; all too soon he must take the very Long Sleep. I hope with all my heart that his gallant little soul may find its Door into Summer, where catnip fields abound and tabbies are complacent, and robot opponents are programmed to fight fiercely —but always lose—and people have friendly laps and legs to strop against, but never a foot that kicks.

Ricky is getting fat, too, but for a temporary happier reason. It has just made her more beautiful and her sweet eternal *Yea!* is unchanged, but it isn't comfortable for her. I'm working on gadgets to make things easier. It just isn't very *convenient* to be a woman; something ought to be done and I'm convinced that some things can be done. There's that matter of leaning over, and also the backaches—I'm working on those, and I've built her a hydraulic bed that I think I will patent. It ought to be easier to get in and out of a bathtub than it is too. I haven't solved that yet.

For old Pete I've built a "cat bathroom" to use in bad weather —automatic, self-replenishing, sanitary, and odorless. However, Pete, being a proper cat, prefers to go outdoors, and he has never given up his conviction that if you just try *all* the doors one of them is bound to be the Door into Summer.

You know, I think he is right.